Christmas Eve Celebration

Christmas Eve Celebration

A DIALOGUE

Friedrich Schleiermacher

A Revised Translation,
with Introduction and Notes by
Terrence N. Tice

CASCADE *Books* • Eugene, Oregon

CHRISTMAS EVE CELEBRATION
A Dialogue

Cascade Books
An Imprint of Wipf and Stock Publishers
199 W. 8th Ave., Suite 3
Eugene, OR 97401

www.wipfandstock.com

ISBN 13: 978-1-60608-961-3

Cataloging-in-Publication Data

Schleiermacher, Friedrich, 1768–1834.
    [Weihnachtsfeier : ein gespräch. English]
    Christmas Eve celebration : a dialogue / Friedrich Schleiermacher ; a
revised translation with introduction and notes by Terrence N. Tice.

    ISBN 13: 978-1-60608-961-3

    Note: A translation of Friedrich Schleiermacher's *Die Weihnachtsfeier: Ein
Gespräch*, Erste und Zweite Ausgabe (Berlin, 1806, 1826)

    xxxii + 114 p. ; 21 cm.—Includes bibliographic references and index.

    1. Theology. 2. Christmas stories. 3. Christian life—Fiction. I. Tice,
Terrence N. II. Title.

BV4515 .S34413 2010

Contents

Editor's Foreword

Schleiermacher is the only major theologian to produce a distinctive book on Christmas for the general public. Although in some ways the work reflects deep theological insight and philosophical acumen, it is not strictly a scholarly work. As a spontaneous testimony of faith, it blends brief explanations with outright celebrations of the Redeemer's birth. The dialogue and stories, the singing, the speeches and nonverbal actions are all placed within the setting of an ordinary German household on Christmas Eve. There women's contributions are highlighted, as are those of a young girl, significantly complementing, even correcting, the more academic presentations among all the men save one. In 1806 this little book was the offering of a seasoned preacher who had already risen to prominence in that role—also as a philosopher, theology professor, and translator of Plato. It is his greatest and final experimentation with fiction as well.

Repeated calls for this work, previously titled *Christmas Eve* for short, and out of print several years now, have led me to revise my 1967 and 1990 editions, originally published by John Knox Press and Edwin Mellen Press. Presented here is a critical version of this translation of the second edition (1826), further textual notes from the 1806 edition, and augmented interpretive material.

Editor's Introduction

I

It is Christmas Eve. The setting is an unpretentious German household, decked with flowers and illumined with the subdued glow of lamps and candles. In the intimate circle of family friends gathered there spirits are bright, if pensive, and the atmosphere of the love and joy of Christmas pervades their being together. The mood is less agitated and the décor less gaudy than is customary today. Gaiety is punctuated with serene expectation and wonder. Most of the action consists of conversation, interspersed with much sudden laughter and with singing. Further, as beseems a quiet celebration of the Redeemer's birth, it all centers in the dancing eagerness, the honest enthrallment, and the tenderness of a child.

Schleiermacher called the piece a dialogue. It is almost a drama, with its own proper staging, the lights and shadows, the dramatis personae, and the interplay of images, words, sound effects, and movement. Yet, it is more an improvisation of inter-mingled moods and themes than an acted story. The real plot lies with the reader, who is not told. As in an exchange of gifts, half of what one receives one brings. Thus, the dialogue is not among the characters alone. It is with the reader too.

Conceived in "a sudden inspiration," the whole work was written and sent to the printer during the three weeks before Christmas, 1805—and this in the midst of a heavy schedule of lecturing. The idea of a dialogue came naturally to mind. Schleiermacher had already experimented with the form twice before, and he had by then published half of his famous six-volume translation of Plato's dialogues. The rest tumbled out of the deep, poignant uncertainty and suffering he had experienced in recent months, now finding release in an ordered expression of faith. Meant especially for his friends and thus written like most of the other major works of his earlier years—as an open, unembarrassed sharing of his personal feeling—the dialogue easily found form. That its elements are astoundingly well knit, despite whatever minor flaws attend its rapid composition, can be attributed only to the genius and conversational ease of its author. The idea of it came to him as he returned to his bachelor's quarters from a concert of the blind flutist Dulon, during the late winter evening of December 2. On the morning before Christmas, he delivered the last pages into the printer's hands.

For Schleiermacher, writing was most satisfactory as an act of personal communication. Conversation, preaching, and lecturing were his most precious arts, in that order of preference; correspondence and other written expressions were but second best. He was far from favoring rhetoric to reason, however. Probably no one in his century had a more well-rounded, less flimsily contrived, gender-inclusive outlook on life than he. Both theologically and philosophically grounded, this general outlook was under constant surveillance and revision. Yet, its grand features remained fairly constant throughout his career; and it informed all his written work, accruing more clarity and cohesiveness as the years went by. Here we find him a still developing scholar of thirty-seven, with all the basic reflection behind him but much critical reconsideration and filling out ahead, so we should not lay more weight on this occasional work than it deserves. The volume certainly does not relay the core message of his theology, nor is it even a systematic explanation of Christmas. Nonetheless, it stands very well on its own merits, as is shown by his willingness to reissue it, only slightly revised, a full twenty years later.

In retrospect, four interlocking factors in Schleiermacher's life seem to have provided the occasion for a dialogue on the celebration of Christmas. The best way to get at them is through his letters. On November 26, 1805, he wrote to his close friend, Ehrenfried von Willich, that in spending "a wonderful hour" with his closest Halle friend, Henrik Steffens, he had felt "embraced within me the deepest pain and the purest joy." Then he immediately went on to say: "Yes, dear brother, I very profoundly feel that as myself I no longer really exist; I am instead the organ of so much that is beautiful and holy, the burning focus from which all the joys and sorrows of my beloved friends radiate. And that I take note of within me, and therefore I live on."[1] On October 25, he had written to Georg Reimer: "my calling and my friends, those are the two hinges on which my life turns."[2]

That month, Henriette von Willich (who, upon Ehrenfried's death, became Schleiermacher's wife four years later) had given birth to her first child (the Steffenses were expecting a similar event early in the new year); and he had written her on the 18th: "I feel joy deep down in the midst of my unhappiness, but as yet I have no words for it."[3] On December 21, only four days before his manuscript was to be finished, he wrote Georg Reimer again: "What I must give up, as Eleanore must, is marriage, the forming of a wholly undivided life . . . Thus, I cannot but keep on saying that I shudder at my life as before an open wound that cannot

1. Heinrich Meisner, editor, *Friedrich Schleiermacher als Mensch: Sein Werke—Familien—und Freundesbriefe, 1804 bis 1834* (Stuttgart: Perthes, 1923), 48. For earlier letters, see Meisner's companion volume: *Schleiermacher als Mensch: Sein Werden—Familien—und Freundesbriefe, 1783 bis 1804* (Stuttgart: Perthes, 1922).

2. Heinrich Meisner, editor, *Friedrich Schleiermacher als Mensch: Sein Werke—Familien—und Freundesbriefe, 1804 bis 1834* (Stuttgart: Perthes, 1923), 46.

3. Heinrich Meisner, editor, *Friedrich Schleiermachers Briefwechsel mit seiner Braut* (Gotha: Perthes, 1919), 53.

be healed, but peace dwells within my heart, dear friend, whole and unalloyed—a peace which, whenever it comes, is by its very nature eternal and cannot wither away."[4]

Finally, before the flute concert on December 2, he wrote to Charlotte von Kathen about his loss of Eleanore. He said that apart from his half-sister Nanny, who was keeping house for him, no one in Halle knew of it but Henrik Steffens. He acknowledged the handwork she had sent him for his birthday on November 21 (nearly all the gifts had been handmade); and he expressed the hope that the suffering she was then undergoing with a sick child would soon be over. It is basically her story that he has Karoline tell in the dialogue. Later he wrote her (June 20, 1806): "You and your precious baby were so involved in the conception of the whole that I could not possibly have failed to bring you into it. Furthermore, my craft knows no finer achievement than that of entwining the lovely strands of mind and heart that have unfolded before me in the lives of others."[5]

The major precipitating factors, then, were these: first, the longing for marriage and a home, which had been aroused to a pitch and shattered by Eleanore; second, the profound peace and joy that permeated through the sharp pain of loss; third, the vicarious identification of his own life with that of his friends, and particularly at that moment with the delight and sorrow they were experiencing with their infant children; finally, the immersion of all his hopes for the future in the twofold calling of preaching and teaching. No wonder that the dialogue has been thought to strike such fundamental chords of human life, and that its open, "romantic" sentimentality seems to have weathered a century and a half of changing moods and tastes.

---

4. Heinrich Meisner, editor, *Schleiermacher als Mensch: Sein Werke—Familien—und Freundesbriefe, 1804 bis 1834* (Stuttgart: Perthes, 1923), 49–50.

5. Ibid., 63.

Little more need be said about the external facts of his situation. From early 1799, Schleiermacher had gone through a deep, mutual, but unconsummated love affair with Eleanore Grunow, she a trapped victim of an early marriage, indecisive in her intention to obtain a divorce. He had patiently waited as she wavered against her basic resolve, and in 1802 he had terminated his six years' residence in Berlin partly to relieve her of any undue pressure. In October 1805, she had finally broken off the relationship, just at the moment when he thought that his hopes were about to be fulfilled. Over a month later (in the November 26 letter quoted above) he was writing to a friend that the "embers" of pain still glowed inside day and night and only hard work would keep them down. The preaching post that he was to assume was not yet available, so he was spending nearly all his working hours on his lectures. That winter term he offered a revised course on ethics and, for the first time, courses on Christian doctrine and Galatians. The latter was to be the first in a study of Paul's writings to parallel his work on Plato, but subsequent duties prevented its completion. Every Friday evening, from seven until after midnight, he had some of his students in for tea. At least one evening a week he went to the Reichardts' home for music. He spent some of the other evenings and Sundays with friends. But nearly every other waking hour—and he typically got along with little sleep—was devoted to either lecturing or study.

II

Where did the young professor come from, and where was he going? Born on November 21, 1768, he was third in a line of Reformed pastors on both sides of the family. Most of his early education was informal; and even his four late-teen years in Herrnhuter Brethren schools granted considerable freedom, in a genuinely communal setting. Both there and at the University of Halle, where he was in residence two years, he concentrated especially on classical studies, philosophy, and theology, which were to become the trivium of his academic career. After passing his theology examinations in 1790, he served as tutor in a noble household for three years. In 1793 and 1794, he did some further teaching in Berlin, joined the Gedike seminar for teacher training, and took further examinations qualifying him for a preaching position. His first pastorate was at Landsberg, between 1794 and 1796. By the time he reached Berlin in the fall of 1796, he was an extraordinarily mature, experienced man of culture for his twenty-seven years. Most of the basic questions and attitudes of his life's course had been firmly established, if only in some respects inchoately.[6] The following six years he served as preacher at Charité Hospital in Berlin, work that gave him time to enter into the cultured circles of the great Prussian city and to do his own first serious writing. Two years as a pastor in Stolpe followed before he accepted his first university appointment, in Halle in 1804.

During that eight-year period in Berlin and Stolpe, between the ages of twenty-seven and thirty-five, he produced the first editions of his most famous popular works, the discourses *On Religion* (1799) and *Soliloquies* (1800). He also translated two volumes of sermons by the Englishman Joseph Fawcett (1798); contributed to the *Athenäum*, an organ of the new "Romantic" school of German literature (1796–1798); wrote a fair-sized book on love and marriage (1800) and a shorter piece on current debate about theology, politics, and the Jews (1799)—both of the latter in the form of letters; produced several lengthy reviews in the areas of philosophy and literature; published his first volume of sermons (1801); put out a nearly five-hundred-page philosophical treatise, *Baselines for a Critique of Previous Works on Ethics* (1803); and issued a two-hundred-page essay

6. For more details, see chapter 1 of my little book *Schleiermacher,* Abingdon Pillars of Theology (Nashville: Abingdon, 2006), xv.

on church-state relations in Prussia (1804). Two large volumes of Plato translations, with introductions, were published in 1804 and another in 1805. Immediately on the heels of his Christmas book came a critical-exegetical work on 1 Timothy and a philological-philosophical study on Heraclitus, both about two hundred pages in length (1807). From 1807 through 1809 he was carrying out a regular correspondence with his future bride, which, since its publication in 1919, has become a classic of its kind, and which is full of the ideas introduced in *Christmas Eve Celebration*. Finally, in 1808 his second volume of sermons appeared, alongside his famous essay on the idea of a German university, which led to his appointment as the first professor of theology in the newly founded University of Berlin that year.

Listing this amazing output gives only a very rough-sketched perspective over the various concerns that had come to dominate Schleiermacher's reflections by the time he wrote *Christmas Eve Celebration* (*Weihnachtsfeier*). In a way, that book arises like a buoyant interlude in the midst of heavy scholarly effort. Moreover, it was, in fact, the first and last purely popular literary work that he ever did. The remainder of his life was largely given over to his regular preaching and other duties at Trinity Church in Berlin, to the teaching of theology and occasionally of philosophy at the University, to his work at the Berlin Academy of Sciences, and to the affairs of politics, church life, and education in his native Prussia. By the time of his death at age sixty-five in 1834, he had become an international figure. It was rightly said that he had inaugurated a new epoch in the history of Christian thought. *Christmas Eve Celebration* stands very much in the middle of this development. This occurred, however, not as a watershed in the man's thought, which followed an extraordinarily smooth course of growth over the years. Rather, it presents a standout symbol for what was most inwardly precious to the man himself: the love and joy that may be known in the Christian life.

III

Much that Schleiermacher wanted to communicate here could be expressed in contexts far removed from the Christmas season. Yet, even the smallest element is quite appropriately viewed with respect to his own confrontation with the Christmas event and his own understanding of its meaning for the world. For him, the coming of the Christ child meant the beginning of a new world—the Word of God become flesh, and we beheld him (John 1:14), for the redemption of all humanity and for the transformation of human society. His firm belief that European religion and culture must undergo radical renewal in the generations ahead, a crucial and broadening renewal perhaps overshadowing even the Reformation age, was set in the larger perspective afforded by that universal event. Probably, the remarkable stability of his life and thought is largely attributable to this vision of faith.

At this point in his life, his systematic evaluation of Christian faith had only just begun. The dialogue itself is open ended and free. It does not preach. Nevertheless, his conviction that Christmas was, and is, the beginning of new things for humanity is basic to the whole. Even a scoffer's words, like Leonhardt's here or worse, could become for him a sign of the new age into which we have all been born through the birth of the world's Redeemer.

For most of the world, the theological tenor of Schleiermacher's main theme is hidden—like the manger in little Sophie's crèche. For this reason, and because theology is only a mode of explanation, not a substitute for human life, the theme must be stated as far as possible in nontheological terms. It is, purely and simply, the commingling of love and joy—not love alone, not joy alone, but joy's accompaniment of love and love's arousal of joy. What this theme signifies in detail can be gathered from the text. A few initial observations may throw light on why the two are so often mentioned, or implied, as a pair within the dialogue.

First, love is a relationship, a state of being; joy is a mood, a state of mind. An interesting clue to this distinction is embedded in ordinary English usage. One can say "I am in love," but "I am in joy" sounds strained. Similarly, one can report, "I was in pain," or "I was in ecstasy" (states of being), but not "I was in joy" (a state of mind). Usage is not entirely consistent, doubtless in part because the line between states of being and states of mind cannot be strictly drawn. We see a difference between being in a bodily state of pain and feeling sorrow, for example, but we would be hard pressed to draw a definite line. Still, if someone is said to live "in sorrow," we take this to indicate that his whole being is affected by sorrow. In such an instance, we are disposed to think of sorrow as something or other, like pain, which has been inflicted on one, or that one inflicts on oneself, but also as a burden one carries. It is not really so much a state of being as something added onto one's course of life. Further, many come to feel that sorrow can be borne if there is also joy. This is so, for joy may come as a gift, a surprise; but it is not something added on. It permeates our whole being and is supreme over all other moods and states. Joy overruns pain and sorrow, fear and anxiety, hate and loneliness. Consequently, while pleasure is something we take or feel, and there is no joy without pleasure, we usually consider joy to be something greater and finer. Joy, in its fullest sense, is the most elevated mood a person can experience. It is virtually synonymous with inner peace, happiness, and fulfillment.

When the mood of joy is viewed in this light, we see why Schleiermacher should couple it with love. That is to say, in his belief, joy is the supreme concomitant of love, and there is no real joy in one's life without love. There might be enjoyment, perhaps, pleasure of a sort; but there would not be real joy, because without love in one's life there is no real cause for rejoicing. The esthete, the nature-lover, the philanderer, and the ecstatic may sometimes get a bigger thrill out of life than others do; but without love their pretended joy is shallow. They have not really learned how to celebrate. Personal well-being may, of course, be an admixture of many things. It is not a product of love alone, nor is joy. Schleiermacher seems to be contending only that joy is extremely partial and momentary—a passing mood—where one's life is shorn of love or lacks at least the memory of love and a trusting in the love of other persons.

Participants in the dialogue deal with this dual theme in a variety of ways. Its basic meaning, however, persists throughout, particularly in the less guarded speech of the women and in the culminating remarks of Eduard and Josef. The celebration of Christmas is also demonstrated and defended in diverse fashion, and yet one fundamental chord remains through it all: Christmas is the supreme festival of joy, because in the birth of Jesus, in that very human act and scene, God displayed God's love for humankind. "Look at it as you will," Schleiermacher seems to be saying; "this is the heart of the matter." Yet, most of his communication is indirect, and we most certainly do it an injustice to sum it up so neatly. It is indirect, above all, because he is trying to intimate the love of God through the love of people. Even at the manger scene, the light shines not only on the babe but on Mary his mother as well. Human love is present in the propagation of the "good news" from the very start.

Nietzsche once said: "A Buddhist acts differently from a non-Buddhist; a Christian acts like everybody else and practices a Christianity of moods and rituals."[7] If overdrawn, the point is nonetheless well taken. Here the primary mood is joy, out of love. The center of the dialogue is, in a way, the account of baptism, where love and joy converge upon the life of a child thence to stream out from the child again. Not detachment, but shared joy and community are the principal ideals of life. Schleiermacher

7. Quoted from Friedrich Nietzsche's *Sämmtliche Werke* XV, 282, in Karl Jaspers, *Nietzsche and Christianity*, Gateway edition (Chicago: Regnery, 1961), 47.

recognizes that Christian experience is never pure wretchedness or pure joy. There is always that "tugging sadness and longing" (*Wehmuth*) within it, which Karoline mentions: a mood compounded of both dignity and self-sufficiency (*Stolze* and *Demuth*), of the finite and the infinite.[8] There is always community and lack of community—that is the human and the Christian lot. The rebirth represented in the communal ritual of baptism is not an alteration of one's nature—"a Christian acts like everybody else"—but a transformation of one's life.

IV

Other themes to look for include the following:

(1) The interplay of jest and earnestness is drawn partly from the Socratic manner but baptized within the context of Christian community. Contemporary readers must be especially wary not to take the bantering too seriously. It is not cruel; it is playful, but honest and considerate. Even the characters have to warn one another, however. People are so easily hurt. Schleiermacher was tremendously sensitive to this fact. He was a master of polemic directed toward the life of the church. Some is subtly introduced here. However, he practiced a gentler, more constructive kind than we find, for example, in Kierkegaard's *Attack on Christendom*. This was partly due to temperament, partly due to his convictions about human relationship.

(2) Musical motifs run all the way through. As an expression of Christian feeling, music is given first place among the arts. Its relation to speech, however, is like the relation between love and joy. Our ability to let music speak for us depends on a communication of truth already haven taken place. Music is not a substitute for proclamation and sharing. Nevertheless, there is something in music more akin to silence than to talking.

8. See *Christian Faith* (§120.P.S.) and *On Religion* II, endnote 14, and V, endnote 14, for accounts of this almost-untranslatable *Wehmuth*.

Max Picard has written: "At the end of the Platonic dialogues it is always as though silence itself were speaking. The persons who were speaking seem to have become listeners to silence."[9] It is the same with Schleiermacher's dialogue. At the end, Josef's plea is for silence, accompanied by song, for something beyond the borderlines of speech and speculation yet, as Schleiermacher would say, difficult to recognize or to experience deeply without them. The theme of peace and conflict is also present in this dialogue, as throughout Schleiermacher's thought, and he strives for peace; but his love of music must not be taken as a sign of preference for harmony at any cost.

(3) Other themes focus on the lineaments of love: marriage and the home, baptism and the education of children, the individual and the communal, the relation between men and women—notably the latter. The relative status of men and women has greatly changed, even in parts of European society, since Schleiermacher's day. Many of the insights about their relations expressed here can be seen to be true, nonetheless, with only slight modification to fit our new circumstances.

Of prime importance is his understanding of love itself, especially of love between a man and a woman. To clarify his view, again in nontheological terms, it is useful to refer back to an earlier work, written in reaction to pious criticism of a romance by his friend Friedrich Schlegel in 1800.[10] The spirituality of human love, Schleiermacher was saying there, is not lost by its becoming physical and direct. Rather, it is thereby fulfilled.

> The so-called religion of love and its divinization was inconsummate, and must thus go under like any other element of old-fashioned religion and culture . . . Pleasure and joy, and the involvement of the body in human life,

9. Picard, *The World of Silence*, Gateway edition (Chicago: Regnery, 1961), 9.

10. Schleiermacher, *Vertraute Briefe über Friedrich Schlegel's Lucinde*, in Schleiermacher, *Sämmtliche Werke* III.1, 482.

are no longer to be regarded as the isolated work of a peculiar "divinity," but as something that can be one with the profoundest and holiest of feelings, with the blending and uniting of the two halves of human nature into a mystical whole. Who cannot thus peer into the very inner reality of divinity and humanity and fathom the mysteries of this quite different religious awareness is not worthy to be a citizen of the new world.[11]

As we see there, for Schleiermacher love is not a disembodied ideal. It is the mutual involvement of persons. Without it, a person's nature is divided in two. One then cannot become a whole person. He is not, of course, speaking only of the "romantic" love between a man and a woman, but of all love. Love is a relationship. In love the physical is not relegated to a lower realm, totally separate from the spiritual life. Our senses and emotions are not an unnecessary part of it; nor is the body unholy.

This view of human love, which Schleiermacher never abandoned, is important for understanding both the arrangement of the *Christmas Eve Celebration* dialogue and its message. The discourse is shared between the men and the women together, even when they contribute stories and speeches separately. They talk together about love of many kinds—of the betrothed, of husband and wife, of parents and children. They compare a man and a woman's point of view; and they differ with each other on these matters, as we will occasionally differ with them. What is most significant, however, is not the comparisons, and not the differences, but the unity these people actually find as they are together in this way. As Schleiermacher insisted in the earlier work, men and women must speak together of love, each in one's own way.[12] Here he fills his own prescription in the setting of a Christian home.

11. Ibid.
12. For example, ibid., 440.

(4) Not so much themes, perhaps, as more casual elements in the dialogue are several other noteworthy factors. According to custom, the adults here occasionally address each other as "children." They know each other very well and are perfectly comfortable in one another's presence, like children. The interplay of language is elegant, but for that none the less genuine and childlike. This fits in nicely with Schleiermacher's view of religious communication, which must be as personal as can be, given the circumstances; and such becomes a minor topic within the dialogue exchange, which is itself an example of religious communication.

Celebration itself is another note, perhaps not so casual after all. Not only is celebration talked about in numerous ways. It is also done. Christmas is really celebrated by the company of the dialogue. In some respects, attending to the manner of celebration may be more revealing of Schleiermacher's meaning and intent than the whole interspersion of talk. The major motifs of the dialogue would have been well enough indicated had the men's interpretations of Christmas never been added. As it is, they represent an intellectual complement, a dialectical counterpart, to the moods and attitudes already expressed in real dialogue and celebration. What makes reflection on the important themes of human existence possible is the concrete, communal history of human beings. What makes reflection on the meaning of Christmas possible is the Christmas story and its coming true for people in their own particular situations. Explanation is an addendum. It comes at the end. Or rather, it fits in just before the end, where the actual story of human life picks up again, as in the concluding remarks of Josef. The Christmas story itself is paramount, together with the stories of people who have come to participate in its reality under the conditions of their own life.

Here there is even one small grace note of politics. The great "destiny," or fate, mentioned by Leonhardt and again referred to in Schleiermacher's preface to the second edition, is the threat of Napoleon's armies, which in1805, sweeping across the western German territories, entered Halle in October of 1806 and overran Prussia soon afterward. This was preying constantly on Schleiermacher's mind. He could not let his cozy Christmas Eve gathering leave the world completely outside. Such, as it happens, was also his view of the church. The world was not outside.

(5) Finally, there is the many-splendored theme of Christmas itself, conjoining and placing its stamp on all the other themes. The reader will want to search this one out for oneself. However, a few preliminary remarks about the way the interpretation of Christmas is handled might be of help.

First of all, only in the last of the four sections, where the men give their extempore speeches, do we find anything like a formal doctrinal statement on the meaning of Christmas. Even here the intent is clearly to relate differing impressions, not to provide a summary account. A full seventy percent of the dialogue is taken up with other means. First a Christmas celebration is described, with all the trappings. Then celebration elides into informal discussion on numerous themes suggested by the Christmas event. In the early evening hours, the child Sophie moves in and out among the adult company like a shuttle on a loom, forming the fabric of their discourse. Eventually, in the third section, her innocent, disarming replies to the catechizing of Leonhardt lead them into a discussion about children; and then the women relate personal incidents, which illumine the time-honored truth that Christmas is a festival for children, a season when adults themselves are able to be children again. A great many insights about Christmas are packed into these few pages, but the method of portrayal is not strictly theological. Doctrinal points are made, or insinuated, but this occurs only as a function of quite informal personal testimony. The reader must fill out the theological implications for oneself.

Where is Schleiermacher himself speaking? Most commentators have agreed that he is not to be identified with any one character. Nor do any of the men seem to correspond directly with any of his friends, though originals for Sophie and for several of the women can be roughly identified. As a rule of thumb, it can be stated that Schleiermacher would be able to assimilate almost everything that the women seriously hold to his own view of things, and that nothing said by Eduard anywhere in the dialogue is inconsistent with his own views at the time. Although he makes Eduard present a far more singular, speculative, compressed Christology than he ever offered himself, Eduard's construction is basically along lines that Schleiermacher was to develop in *Christian Faith* (1821–1822; revised 1830–1831). Nor can the categories and formulations offered in the dialogue be significantly identified with the theological position of any well-known contemporary.

Ernst does not really present a clear, outright position. He has taken more the stance of an apologist, whom one has to second-guess. He places the essence of the festival in the religious connection of our life with Christ's, and he elevates joy, as Schleiermacher would do (though in a one-sided omission of any reference to love); but the many gaps in his picture seem to require the ordering brush of Eduard. Most of his earlier conversation (about marriage, music, and personal growth) also gives the impression of a young man rather too bold and dogmatic, yet one set upon a path of which Schleiermacher would generally approve. Leonhardt is a horse of a different color. He is certainly a most charming, scintillating fellow. He is out to trounce dogmatists. He has a good heart, and he dwells not far outside the fold of faith. Clearly Schleiermacher is very fond of this character and is sympathetic to many of his critical views about Christianity. He has made him his spokesman against the narrow-minded. However, great care must be taken even when, as a confessed nonbeliever, Leonhardt expresses very similar viewpoints to Schleiermacher's own, not to identify them too closely with positions that Schleiermacher himself would hold as a believer. Even historical questions may be seen from a different perspective on opposite sides of the fence—questions about the figure of Jesus above all. When in doubt, the reader will do well to see what Eduard has to say.

Knowing about Schleiermacher's recent history leaves us no hesitation about Josef. He is all Schleiermacher. The entire evening he has been roaming about sharing in the joy of his friends, just as Schleiermacher might have envisaged doing himself on the eve of the day he penned that last scene in which Josef suddenly appears. Josef jokingly rejects the dry dissection of Christmas that he surmises must have been going on with Leonhardt sitting there. He draws the company back to that joyful reality of new life and community in Christmas, which no words can capture. He calls them to silence—a filled silence, with a firm background of proclamation and sharing, a silence broken out into song.

V

Schleiermacher's *Christmas Eve Celebration* was first translated by W. Hastie (Edinburgh: T. & T. Clark, 1890). Here and there a felicitous expression has been adopted from that earlier edition, but the present text was already a wholly new translation, using the truncated title, in 1967. Hopefully, it presents fewer traces of turgidity and a fair reduction of faulty and misleading expressions. At any rate, the aim has been to give as current a ring to the language as possible without divorcing it from Schleiermacher's own precise meaning and style. It follows the critical edition of Hermann Mulert, *Friedrich Schleiermachers Wiehnachtsfeier*, Philosophische Bibliothek 117 (Leipzig: Dürr, 1908), which presents the first edition of 1806 with all second-edition changes carefully indicated in notes. Here, however, the procedure is reversed.

The long paragraphs have been broken up; exclamation points and other devices, such as placing headings with the names of characters who are about to tell a story or make a speech, have also been employed to highlight the dialogue character of the book, following clues clearly indicated in the German text. Otherwise the main text exactly corresponds to the second edition of 1826. The pages of that edition are dotted with minor alterations, but a careful comparison reveals that nearly all of the some 328 changes are stylistic. Most of the remainder were obviously inserted for purposes of clarification or slight expansion. Only the bulk of Leonhardt's views on the significance of religious festivals and on the relation of the atonement to Christmas, and of Ernst's remarks on the universal import of Christmas were substantially rewritten. The latter editing replaces some unpropitious expressions in the first edition, and it presents elucidation of several points inadequately made; but it shifts the original impression very little. This finding corroborates Schleiermacher's own judgment expressed in the preface to the 1826 edition.

The table of contents, the brief description of the dramatis personae, the notes, the headings, and the index are the responsibility of the present editor alone, though some information in the notes originated with Hermann Mulert. Thanks are due to friends and family for consultation on minutiae of the translation. They would also no doubt share in the hope that this little "gift," as Schleiermacher called it, might help supply a more meaningful approach to the celebration of Christmas in other households, as it has in their own.

A literal translation of the German title reads: "Christmas Eve Celebration: A Dialogue," used in this edition. Two important aspects of Schleiermacher's title are lost in such a transcription. In the earlier two editions, the more hidden but nonetheless basic aspect was retained in the title, aptly suggested by John Knox Press: the implicit reference to the incarnation.

By this is simply meant the coming into being of a man, who is the world's Redeemer (in traditional shorthand: his becoming "flesh," though, in Schleiermacher's view, not a preexistent Logos, or Word). While this is not a strictly theological book, there would be little point in producing a dialogue on Christmas where a profound conviction concerning the unique importance of Jesus's birth for the world was absent. Schleiermacher carries the incarnational idea further than many theologians have, by stressing what Jesus's sharing of his life with others unto death has actually effected within the human community. The intimate gathering of family and friends depicted in this book is thus a paradigm of hope for the entire family of humankind. From early times, Christmas has been, with Easter, one of the two great festivals of the church. The German term for Christmas is, literally, "Holy Night." The festival of Christmas, sacred or secular, is thereby unmistakably centered on Christmas Eve. Yet as Schleiermacher's little drama shows, what is celebrated at Christmas goes far beyond the manger scene itself. Its scope is the whole history and destiny of humanity.

The second aspect, which translation can only awkwardly portray, is the note of celebration. The word *celebration* was initially missing from our title. There seemed to be no graceful way to keep it in. Restoring it here recaptures the primary mood Schleiermacher hoped to convey. Christmas is, as Ernst says, the supreme "festival of joy."

Terrence N. Tice
Denver, Colorado
February 2010

Dramatis Personae

Ernestine—the lady of the fairly typical cultured household
in which the entire action takes place—knowing,
intelligent, pure hearted, superbly feminine

Eduard—the host, Ernestine's husband, a serenely religious
man, theologically astute and experienced in church
affairs; the two are very close in their views and
feelings

Sophie—their precocious, energetic young daughter, of perhaps
ten or eleven: devoted to religious music, and as
wholly wrapped up in the Christmas festivities as in
everything that strikes her childish fancy; her figure
is a prism for much of the evening's activities and
discussions

Anton—Agnes's child, not so old as Sophie, just getting his
schoolbooks; after the beginning, the presence of
Anton and of his younger brother fades out of the
story

Leonhardt—a jovial, crisp-thinking lawyer, the youngest of the
men; he is not much of a churchgoer, but more of a
believer than some give him credit for; he holds very
critical, rationalistic views about Christianity; Josef
calls him an "evil principle" for such a gathering, a
"dialectical, superintellectual man"

Friederike—a sparkling, clever young woman, engaged to
marry Ernst; she is partial to the poems of Novalis and
is especially gifted at improvising on the piano

Ernst—Friederike's enthusiastic bridegroom, a devout man
possessed of a speculative sense for the symbolic in
history

Karoline—an unmarried woman: ready to defend the cause of
        her sex, vivacious, and quick to take up an argument—
        especially against Leonhardt

Agnes—a thoughtful, deep-feeling mother of two boys, now
        expecting another

Josef—an unidentified friend who arrives late, after an evening
        of merrymaking, ebullient with Christmas spirit and
        in a better mood for singing than for discourse

Schleiermacher's Preface to the Second Edition

Times have changed since this little book first appeared nearly twenty-one years ago. The "great forces of destiny"[1] then threateningly advancing have played their role, and the great battle has splintered into a thousand pieces. Even though the religious differences that confront each other here essentially persist, their tone and color have significantly altered, so that most of them no longer have quite the same truth now as they did then.

Yet, these considerations do not seem to me sufficient to support bringing the book out once again. Nor do the few and insignificant emendations I have proposed to make have the aim of adapting it more nearly to the present moment, which would have required the thankless task of reworking the whole text. Rather, they serve only to fasten down and secure what seems to me to have been expressed with insufficient clarity and definiteness, and to do so without disturbing any essential feature.

If similarly varied opinions on these subjects appear to diverge more sharply from each other today, and if in our life within polite and cultivated society we often find cause to regret that people who merit one another's love and influence are completely divided and cut off from one another, perhaps it will be a gratifying view—and one not unworthy to be offered as a Christmas gift—to be shown how the most varied ways of conceiving Christianity may peacefully coexist in an ordinary living room, not by ignoring each other but by amiably engaging each other in common reflection and sharing of views. And so, this little book may hope once again to find a gracious reception and

1. Ed. note: Napoleon's army.

to have its good effect, in that in its own way it serves to remind us that the letter kills but the Spirit alone gives life.[2]

Berlin, end of November, 1826

2. Ed. note: 2 Corinthians 3:6.

1

Christmas Eve

The friendly drawing room was all decked out for Christmas Eve. Flowers had been brought to it from every window ledge in the house. The curtains were kept tied up to let the glistening snow give testimony to the season. Drawings and paintings associated with the holy festival adorned the walls, some a gift of the lady of the household to her husband. The many lanterns hung high above spread a festive light all round, which yet seemed to play tricks with curiosity. Indeed, familiar things showed up clearly enough, but only by unhurried and close attention could one distinctly recognize and duly appreciate[1] what was strange or new there. So had the gay and thoughtful Ernestine arranged it all, that only gradually could one's impatience, aroused half in jest, half in earnest, be satisfied. For still a while, the wee, brightly colored gifts lying about remained carpeted in shimmer.

This time everyone in the intimate circle that was to gather there—the men and women, and the children too—had entrusted to her the task of gathering together all that they had brought for one another's delight, thus grandly conjoining things that would look undistinguished by themselves. Now she had finished. It was as if one were in a winter garden, where one must look carefully among the evergreen shrubs to find the tiny

1. In 1806: "distinctly perceive." Ed. note: In many German territories, over the past three decades celebration of Christmas in church had come to be forbidden, hence the custom of household celebration depicted here.

blossoms of galanthus[2] and violets under blanket of snow or the protective covering of moss. Here each thing was bordered with ivy, myrtle, and amaranthus, and the loveliest things lay hidden under white coverlets or gaily colored cloths, whereas the larger gifts were scattered about the room or had to be sought out under the tables. The initials of each person were inscribed on the wrappings[3] with trifles to eat, and each was then at liberty to try to find out[4] who had given the particular presents.

The whole group waited in the adjoining room, their mirth piqued by impatience. Someone would pretend to guess or to betray what a certain gift was going to be, and would unmistakably insinuate its relation to some minor foible or habit, some funny incident, or some farcical misunderstanding or embarrassment involving present company. Then persons caught by such delicate blows would hasten to return them on all sides.

All the while little Sophie was excitedly pacing about the room in big strides, wrapped up in her own thoughts. As the others jostled about, talking, her restless rhythm of movement was almost as much in their way as they in hers. Finally Anton, with feigned annoyance, asked her whether she would not gladly forgo all her presents for a magic mirror[5] that would allow her to peer behind the closed doors.

"At least," she retorted, "I would be more likely to do that than you, for you are more self-indulgent than curious; and, anyway, you think that the rays of your marvelous wit cannot be stopped by any obstacles!"[6] Whereupon she plunked herself down in the darkest corner and sat there pensively, cradling her head in her upturned palms.

---

2. Ed. note: Snowdrops.

3. *Bedekkungen*; in 1806: *Dekken*.

4. In 1806: "and it was up to each to find out."

5. *Magischen Spiegel*; in 1806: *Glas* ("looking glass").

6. In 1806: "door."

In a short while Ernestine opened the door, and the merry company flocked through as she remained there leaning against it. Yet, instead of rushing eagerly to the bright, laden tables, as would have been expected, when they had reached the middle of the room where the whole scene could be surveyed, all suddenly, automatically[7] turned their gaze to her. The arrangement was so beautifully done and so fully expressed her good taste that their feelings were spontaneously drawn to her, and without a moment's thought their eyes followed. She was standing there half in the shadows, thinking to take delight, unnoticed, in her loved ones and their buoyant joy; but it was she in whom they all first took delight, and they gathered around her as though she had given them everything and they had already enjoyed it to the full. Touched beyond smiling, the child clasped her about the knees and looked up at her, her eyes wide in fondest admiration. The women embraced her. Eduard kissed her lovely downcast eyelid, and in a suitable way each showed her the most hearty love and devotion. She herself had to beckon them on to claim their gifts.

"I am glad if you like the way I have arranged things, my dears," she said; "but please do not forget the picture for the frame. Bear in mind that I have tried only to do honor to the day that we are celebrating and to your own joyful love, the tokens of which you have entrusted to me. Come forth, then, and let all of you see what presents are here for you; and if you cannot guess correctly, may you bear our joshing patiently!"

Of that there was plenty. With great confidence the women called out who had given every one of their presents, and the girls too, so that no one could deny it. The men, however, were often mistaken; and nothing was more amusing—or annoying—than for one of them to flash out a clever guess, only to have it parried under protest, like throwing back the wrong change.

7. "Suddenly, automatically," inserted in 1826.

"We will just have to take it," said Leonhardt, "though it always naturally bothers us that the ladies are so much sharper than we at such precious little things as these! This is so, for the meaning expressed in the presents they give discloses that the most artful attention has been accorded them, and that is more than can be said of ours. Realizing this, and enjoying these pleasant fruits of their talent, we simply have to bear the other result as it comes, even though it puts us somewhat in the shade."

"You are too kind," replied Friederike. "It is not so much our talent that gives us the advantage as, if I may say so, a certain lack of skill on the part of you men. You very much prefer the straightforward way of doing things, as befits the strong and lordly. Thus, while you may not want to divulge anything thereby, your moves are nevertheless as much dead giveaways as the gestures of chess players who cannot keep from touching the troublesome pieces of their opponents and indecisively lifting their own six times over before taking their turn."

"Ah yes," Ernst put in, smiling but feigning a sigh. "It is still true, as old Solomon says, that God hath made man upright, but women have sought out many inventions."[8]

"Then you may at least have the consolation," retorted Karoline, "of knowing that you have not undone us by all your modern good manners.[9] Who knows? Perhaps both qualities are as eternal as they are needful. Moreover, if, as it happens, your forthright simplicity is the occasion of our cunning, then set

8. Ed. note: As I indicated in the 1967 edition, this is a popular misrendering of Ecclesiastes 7:29. However, as Patsch, KGA I/5 (1995) points out, the contrast between men and women was not present either in the Hebrew text or in translations of the time; further, it uses Luther's word *Künste* instead of *Anschläge*, which refers to humans' being created upright (*aufrichtig,* "sincere") but to their being wont to have "designs against" this. The same misunderstanding, which Schleiermacher seems to make into a joke here, is easily derived in English from the wording of both the KJV and RSV.

9. *Artigkeit.*

your mind at rest: the other way around, our less capacious habits may well relate similarly to the talents in which you excel."

Meanwhile, the whole company was inspecting the gifts more closely, and everyone was examining and praising appreciatively the particularly female offerings of knitting and fine needlework. At first, Sophie had thrown only a fleeting glance over her own treasures. She left them so as to weave in and out among the group, peeking curiously at everything and exulting in it all. Above all else, however, she was industriously begging for bits of candied initials on things once they had broken apart, for her appetite for sweets was insatiable, and she liked to save up great stores of them, especially when she could gather them like this. Only after she had swelled her hoard of sweets by this supply did she begin to take more exact stock of her presents; and then she made the rounds again, showing and exclaiming over every one in turn, trying to display each in a way that would most surely demonstrate its excellence.

"But you seem not to have noticed the best of them all," remarked her mother.

"Oh yes, I really have, Mother,"[10] replied the child. "But I have not yet had the heart to open it, for if it is a book, it would be useless to look into it here. Later I must shut myself up in my room to enjoy it first there.[11] Yet, maybe someone—and I am sure it was not you—has made serious sport with me: Maybe someone has given me patterns and directions for all sorts of knitting and sewing and other such marvelous things. If so, I promise you as positively as I can that I will make good use of it in the new year. Just now, though, I would rather not know about it!"

"Poor guess," her father said. "It is not anything like that, nor have you wanted to be in a position to merit having such

10. *Einzige Mutter.* Ed. note: The adjective *einzige* is a way of saying this is her one and only, as would be said of one's beloved.

11. *Erst;* in 1806: *auch* ("as well").

gifts as yet, but neither is it a book that you would have to retire to your room to enjoy properly."

At that she jumped up, suddenly all eagerness—though at the risk of scattering most of her treasures—and exclaimed with a shriek,[12] "Music!" And leafing through what she had found, she said, "Oh, wonderful music! A whole lifetime of Christmases! 'You shall sing, O children of God, the most glorious things.'" Now she was reading the titles of the pieces, which were mostly religious music, all written in celebration of Christmas, all excellent and some old and little known. Whereupon she leapt over to her father, in a burst of gratitude, and covered him with kisses.

Alongside the dislike of women's handicrafts already intimated, the child had shown a decided talent for music, though one limited in scope. Her taste was not at all limited, for she knew hearty enjoyment of everything fine in the art of music. On her own, however, she did not then particularly care to practice pieces not set in the grand style of church music. It was rarely to be taken for a sure sign of a purely joyful mood when she warbled half aloud some light and merry song. When she would sit down to the piano, however, and begin to sing out in her lovely voice, already tending to the lower range, it was this grand genre of music she always chose.[13] Here she knew how to treat each note aright;[14] her touch and phrasing made each chord sound forth with an attachment that can scarcely tear itself from the rest but that then stands forth in its own measured strength until it too, like a holy kiss, gives way to the next. Even when she would sing a part alone, for practice, her singing conveyed[15] so much respect for the other voices that it was as though she were really hearing them too. However deeply moved she may

12. In 1806: "a loud cry."
13. In 1806: "it was always only from this grand genre."
14. In 1806: "to offer each note its due."
15. In 1806: "practice, she conveyed."

often have been, no sort of excess would ever surge up to disturb what harmony belonged to the music as a whole. Apart from the particular music, such performance can hardly be described except to say that she sang with reverence, and cherished each successive tone with humble caring.

Thus, since Christmas is most appropriately the children's festival, and since she herself lived Christmas so remarkably, what present could seem to her more precious than this?

She sat for awhile absorbed in the score, her fingers forming the chords[16] as she studied it. Her gestures and the changing expressions on her face showed that she was singing to herself, without making a sound. Suddenly she sprang up and started across the room, but then turned half about and announced: "Can you leave all your looking and talking for a moment and come upstairs to be my guests? I have already lit the rooms. Tea will soon be ready, too, so now seems the best time. As you know, I was not allowed to make you any presents, but I am not forbidden to invite you to a performance!" The condition had been laid down that she could be admitted among those who gave presents as soon as she was able to produce a neat, flawless piece of handicraft as her first gift. This she had not yet brought off, but she wanted to make amends for it in some way.

Sophie happened to possess one of those little mechanical panoramas designed to represent the story of Christmas by means of tiny carved figures that move within an appropriate setting. Usually the story is as good as lost in a jumble of irrelevant fixtures, some of them tasteless, others a travesty.[17] These accessories are put on to give as flashy a performance as possible with what is actually a very simple mechanism. This display she had tidied up and installed in its new form, adding improvements of her own here and there. Now visitors entering her room were witnesses to a striking scene, erected upon

16. In 1806: "the sounds."
17. In 1806: "irrelevant, tasteless fixtures."

a rather large table[18] and effectively illuminated with candles. Arranged informally about the table, and with tolerable skill, were representations of many of the important moments within the external history of Christianity, only a few episodes dividing them. In the same vicinity, one could see the baptism of Christ, Golgotha and the mount of ascension, or the outpouring of the Spirit, the destruction of the temple, and Christians ranged in battle against the Saracens over the holy sepulcher. In another grouping there was the pope marching in solemn procession to St. Peter's, the martyrdom of Hus, and Luther's burning of the papal bull; in another the baptism of the Saxons, missionaries in Greenland and Africa, a Herrnhuter Brethren churchyard, and the Halle Orphanage. The original designer had apparently wished to give special emphasis to the latter as[19] the most recent great accomplishment of religious zeal. The child had obviously taken pains to employ flame and water throughout the whole composition, making a fine pattern with the two conflicting features.[20] Streams actually flowed, and fires flickered. With great dexterity she had managed to keep the faint flames burning and to protect them.

Now, among all these highlighted objects one sought for a long time in vain for the birth scene itself, for she had wisely contrived[21] to conceal the Christmas star. One had to follow after the angels and after the shepherds gathered around a campfire, then open a door[22] in the wall of the structure—the house having been given only a decorative function—and there in an enclosure, which actually lay out of doors, one looked upon the

18. In 1806: "tidied up, installed, and improved here and there, and now this striking scene was erected upon a rather large table in her room."

19. In 1806: "had apparently regarded this as."

20. In 1806: "throwing the two conflicting features into relief."

21. In 1806: "thought."

22. In 1806: "a door entirely."

holy family. All was dark in the lowly shed, save one beam of light streaming down from some hidden source upon the infant's head and casting a reflection on the bowed face of his mother. In contrast to the wild flames on the other side, this mild splendor seemed like a heavenly over against an earthly light. Sophie herself joined in appraising this with evident satisfaction as her masterpiece. She had imagined herself a second Correggio[23] in doing it, and she now kept her craft a tight secret. Only she did admit that as yet she had schemed in vain over how she might bring in a rainbow too, which she had very much wanted, she explained, for Christ is the true surety that life and pleasure[24] will never more be lost to the world.

For some moments she knelt down before her creation, her little head reaching only up to the table, her gaze fixed upon the tiny chamber. Suddenly she was aware that her mother was standing just behind her, and without shifting she turned to her and exclaimed with deep feeling: "Oh, Mother, you might just as well be the happy mother of the divine babe! And are you perhaps sorry that you are not? And is this, do you suppose, why mothers would rather have boys? But think of the holy women who followed Jesus and of all that you have told me about them. Certainly I will become such a woman some day, will I not, as you are now?" Profoundly moved, her mother lifted her up and embraced her.

Meanwhile, the others were all viewing the various parts of the panorama. Anton was particularly intent. He had his younger brother beside him, and he was pointing out and explaining all that he knew with the verbose and gushing vanity of a tour guide.[25] The smaller fellow looked very attentive, but he

---

23. Ed. note: Reference is to *The Night* (1530), by Correggio (1489–1534), to be found in the Gemäldegalerie in Dresden.

24. *Leben und Lust.*

25. *Cicerone.*

understood nothing and kept wanting to touch the water and the flames to be sure they were real and not an enticing illusion.

While most of the party were still busy looking, Sophie softly persuaded her father to join her, with Friederike and Karoline, in the other room, where Karoline sat down to the piano and the four sang the hymn "Let Us Love Him" and the chorale "Welcome to This Vale of Sorrow." They followed these with some additional[26] things from Reichardt's splendid *Christmas Cantelina*, in which[27] the feeling of deliverance and humble devotion and joy are all so beautifully expressed.[28] Soon the whole company[29] had become their reverent audience, and when they had finished, all remained still, as so often happens with religious music, in a mood of inner satisfaction and retirement. This reaction was followed by a few silent moments in which they all knew[30] that the mind and heart of each person was turned in love toward all the rest and toward something higher still.

26. In 1826 "additional" is inserted.

27. In 1806: "where."

28. Ed. note: Johann Friedrich Reichardt (1752–1814) was a noted composer, and he had been director of church music in Halle during Schleiermacher's years there. At least weekly Schleiermacher had been invited to the home of his highly musical family as their good friend. Reichardt's *Weibmacht-Cantilene von Claudius* had appeared in 1768 and 1792. Both pieces come from this work. See Patsch (KGA I/5, 1995, S. 50) for the original, identical texts of the two chorales, sung to different melodies, one of them traditional. The text: "Welcome to this vale of sorrow, / Oh be welcome a thousandfold, / be blessed a thousandfold, / you dear sweet child. / A cold wind buffets us, and it is snowing, raining here. / We trudge upon our way comfortless and dejected, / much tormented in a strange land, / imprisoned, to the point of death, / and there you come to us in our distress, / to bring us home to our father's house, our father's flock— / we are not worthy of this, / we are not worthy."

29. In 1806: "all."

30. In 1806: "in which each knew."

At the call to tea, all but one soon gathered together again in the drawing room. Sophie remained assiduously working at the piano, and she only darted in and out again, with scarcely a word for anyone, in order to quench her thirst.

2

Christmas Themes

Everyone was milling about, busying themselves once again with the presents. It was only now, after the interruption, that these appeared truly to come into the possession of their new owners. On this account, they were already more detached[1] from their donors now, too, and could be viewed as something not their own and more freely praised. Much had previously been overlooked by several of the party, and the special features of some gifts were only now discovered.

"This year," Ernst pronounced, "is especially favorable for rejoicing in our gifts, for some important changes are coming just ahead. The darling baby things with which Agnes has been so plentifully bestowed; the lovely, delicate jewelry for our future relation, my dear Friederike; the luggage for Leonhardt, even the schoolbooks for your Anton, dear Agnes—all point toward progress and happy times ahead and make future joys vividly present to us in anticipation. Since Christmas is itself the announcement of a new life for the world, naturally its celebration will impress and cheer us most when something new and important is coming up in our own life. I take you in my arms as if you were a new gift to me today, my beloved Friederike. A wonderful festive feeling of supreme joy grips me tonight, as if you had only just now been given to me, along with my Redeemer. Indeed, I am sorry that all of you cannot be devoutly kneeling before such a new stage of life as we are, that for you, my dear friends, nothing is to

1. In 1806: "They were more detached."

be expected of the magnitude approaching the greatest event of all;[2] and I fear that our gifts to you may seem insignificant beside yours to us. Your spirits may be cheerful and happy, if less moved and exalted than ours are—indeed, I might almost say indifferent[3] as compared with our own."

"You are certainly very kind, dear friend," Eduard retorted,[4] "to look upon us so tenderly from out of your obvious rapture! Yet, this very enthusiasm of yours surely places us much too far away from you for comfort. Please consider that our more tranquil happiness is precisely the same as that[5] which you are approaching, and that no genuine exaltation of spirit, including that of love, ever grows old. It can always be aroused anew. Can you regard Ernestine's feeling at our Sophie's expression of childish devotion and piety as something comparatively different? Or isn't it true that you can only look at it with liveliest imagination, in which past, present, and future are all intertwined? Just see how deeply moved she is, in what a sea of purest happiness she bathes."

"Yes, I readily confess it," responded Ernestine. "Her few words have fairly transported me just now. No, I do her an injustice. By themselves these words might well have appeared as affectation to someone who does not know her. All in all, it was the whole perspective[6] of the child that moved me so. Her heart opened up like an angel's, so marvelous and pure. Furthermore, if you understand what I mean, since I do not know how to put

2. In 1806: "this great event."

3. In 1806: "indeed, almost indifferent."

4. In 1806: "said."

5. In 1806: "precisely that."

6. *Anschauung.* Ed. note: Or "perception," which in the original 1799 edition of *On Religion*, and in the 1806 and 1821 editions as well, is often paired with feeling (*Gefühl*) in reference to the two inseparable aspects of what he later called "immediate religious self-consciousness" in *Christian Faith* (1821–22, 1830–31).

it any other way, in her feeling there was such a deep and basic understanding, expressed in such an unrestrained, unconscious way, that I trembled to think what a fullness of beauty and winsomeness must come from it as she grows older. In a certain respect, I truly feel that she did not say too much when she thought that I might well be the mother of the blessed child, because I can in all humility honor the pure revelation of the divine in my daughter, as Mary did in her son, without in the least disturbing[7] the regular[8] relation of mother to child."

"We are all of one mind on that," added Agnes. "Spoiling and pampering springs from love not of one's children but of oneself, from the desire to spare oneself unpleasantness. This can have nothing to do with what you mean."

"We women understand that very well," Ernestine continued. "Yet, on occasion shouldn't we expressly remonstrate with the men on this matter? When it comes to their special concern for[9] the boys, being brave and proficient is the thing, and progress is then always bound up with hard exertion and denial; indeed,[10] it may often be considered necessary to hold down their growing feeling of autonomy. This state of affairs[11] might easily give their fathers[12] a faulty perspective, however, if they do not diligently orient themselves upon our motherly sense and way of doing things!"

At this challenge Eduard spoke up: "Of course, we recognize that you are meant to care for the first pure kernels of childhood and to help them develop before any corruption enters in or gets established. You are made that way. Women who devote

7. In 1806: "without disturbing."

8. *Richtige*; in 1806: *rechte* ("proper").

9. *Sorge . . . für*, in 1806: *Sorge . . . bei* ("with").

10. In 1806: "and."

11. In 1806: "Doing that."

12. In 1806: "them" (i.e. the boys).

themselves to this holy service fittingly dwell within the temple, vestals watching over the sacred fire. In contrast, we must venture forth into the world in strict array, practicing discipline and preaching penance, or as pilgrims cleaving fast to the cross and girding ourselves with swords in order to seek out some sacred object and to recover it."[13]

"You bring me back to a thought that I had almost lost[14] in following the flow of this discussion," broke in Leonhardt. "It concerns your Sophie, and has several times been on the tip of my tongue, but it has come to me quite forcefully now. It is that although her childish piety certainly moves me as well,[15] I am also alarmed by it at times. When her feelings burst out, her spirit sometimes seems to me[16] like a bud that perishes[17] from too forceful an impulse within before it opens. Dear friends, by all that is sacred, do not nourish this feeling overmuch. Maybe you cannot see[18] her so vividly as I do, not far ahead: her colors early faded, veiled and kneeling perhaps before the image of a saint, fingering her rosary in fruitless ardor; or, if not that, then garbed[19] in the revolting little cap and graceless gown of a Herrnhuter sister, no longer at liberty really to enjoy life because she is cloistered off in a Sisters' Home. Imagine her brooding

---

13. Ed. note: See Schleiermacher's *The Christian Household: A Sermonic Treatise,* tr. of the 1820 and 1826 editions, with essays and notes, by Dietrich Seidel and Terrence N. Tice (Lewiston, NY: Mellen, 1991). The nine sermons and other appended texts form a take on roles of men and women at that time in marriage, child rearing, treatment of domestic servants, hospitality, and charity. These 1818 sermons were then rewritten for readers and further revised for clarification.

14. In 1806: "that I had lost"

15. *Ebenfalls*; in 1806: *auch* ("too")

16. In 1806: "sometimes I view her spirit as."

17. In 1806: "is spent."

18. In 1806: "imagine."

19. In 1806: "or in a shabby and ineffectual life, garbed."

away, dull and inactive, in one of those places![20] It is a dangerous time for such things. Many lovely feminine spirits have been swept up in one of these awful mistakes, tearing their family ties asunder. However you look at it, the finest way of life destined for women, and their richest happiness, is foresworn, not to mention that inner perversion of soul without which such things would not happen in the first place. And I am afraid that the child leans heavily in this direction. It would indeed be an irreplaceable loss if that precious soul and spirit of hers should be carried away by the corruption of a time in which, one might almost say, few women[21] have kept their honor entirely unspotted[22]—that is, if what Goethe said is true: that there is always a stain on a person's character when one has, if only in a certain sense or other, given up[23] the marriage relation or changed one's religion.[24] A friend who has such a concern as this should speak it out, but only once; and so it may not have been amiss for me to hold back until today, though I don't know why it was that I did."

"I can testify," said Ernestine, "that you have hesitated, for I have sensed your feeling of concern more than once; and since it is so definite, it might well have passed into words much ear-

20. Ed. note: This sentence represents a phrase added in 1826. This was precisely where Schleiermacher's sister had been living since their years of schooling in Brethren communities, though neither of them would characterize her life there in such negative terms. See note 41 below.

21. In 1806: "in which few women."

22. In 1806: "kept their honor unspotted."

23. In 1806: "when one has given up."

24. Ed. note: Goethe's remark appeared early in 1805: "Indeed," he said, "a kind of permanent stain is marked on anyone who changes his religion. . . . If he stays by his country, his city, his prince, his friend, or his wife . . . that is honored." J. W. von Goethe, *Winckelmann und sein Jahrhundert* (Tübingen, 1805), in *Deutsche National-Litteratur*, edited by Joseph Kürchner, Bd. 108 (*Goethes Werke*, Bd. 27), Abschnitt "Katholizismus," 49–50.

lier. I did not exact it from you, however, because I hoped that you would become suspicious of it yourself when you observed the child more and could see her inner qualities unfolded more clearly. Look at it this way, my dear. Certainly you are correct[25] in supposing that some distortion within always lies at the roots of a person's entering upon such a course of life as you were concerned about. And where is this more easily recognizable than in a child about whom one can have so little doubt as to whether such has really emerged[26] from within or has been acquired only from[27] without? Yet, can you point out anything that is actually distorted in her, anything at all that exceeds the true qualities of childhood?[28] Or is there some circumstance in her life gone awry, whereby something that would otherwise become her is suppressed by her religious impulses? All I know is that she has gone about this just as unreservedly as she goes about anything else that is precious to her. She gives herself to every motivation precisely in this way.[29] With every unquestionably childish interest you will find her behaving just the same;[30] and she truly bears as little vanity with this particular interest as with any other. Furthermore, she has no occasion to fix on this alone, nor will she ever have such an occasion, as far as her parents are concerned, for no one pays it any special attention. Moreover, if she must surely become aware of how very highly we esteem this disposition, yet she will never see us make much of a fuss over particular impulses of this kind or of their expression. We regard her religious interest as perfectly natural; and this disposition does in fact come quite naturally to her. In our way of think-

---

25. *Richtig*; in 1806: *recht* ("right").

26. In 1806: "has emerged."

27. In 1806: "acquired from."

28. In 1806: "in her, that exceeds being a child?"

29. In 1806: "every motivation in this way."

30. In 1806: "behaving the same."

ing, what arises naturally can be left to nature, without further interference on our part."

Half interrupting, Eduard quickly picked up the line of thought. "And indeed all the more surely," said he, "the more all this belongs to what is finest and noblest, for clearly, my dear friend, the right view of the matter must be that this inner something that takes hold of the child so strikingly has no opportunity to attach itself upon anything merely external. This Christmas play will be laid aside in a few days; and you yourself know very well that there is no formalism of a religious sort[31] in our family circle—no prayer at set times, no special hour for private devotions—but that everything like this is done only as the spirit leads. Moreover, she often hears us speaking of such matters, and even singing—of which she is otherwise extremely fond—without joining in; and all this is quite in accord with the manner of children. Generally speaking, she takes no particular pleasure[32] in going to church. She considers the singing poor. The rest[33] of the service she does not understand, and it bores her. Were there anything forced in her piety, or were she inclined to mimic others or to let herself be led by external authority, would she not then compel herself to approve of what we so conspicuously hold in respect and consider it worthy of her participation? Now, I think all this fits in so well with the rest of her development that I cannot see how the Roman or even the Herrnhuter way of life could ever attract her. In fact, before this could happen, she would have to put completely aside[34] her own distinctive sense of value,[35] which has this character not at all;

---

31. *Nichts förmliches Religiöses.*
32. In 1806: "of children. She takes no special pleasure at all."
33. In 1806: "poor. Moreover, the rest."
34. In 1806: "would have to lose."
35. *Eigenthümlichen Geschmack.*

and she would have to rid herself entirely of[36] her almost blunt, audacious way[37] of distinguishing in everything between what is primary and what is only a semblance or appurtenance."

Before Leonhardt could reply, Karoline chimed in: "If it were up to me, I should like to forbid you to throw[38] Herrnhuter and Roman piety into one basket like this. I think one could question whether the two are the same in any respect whatsoever; but at the very least I cannot allow your fancy word, 'perversion,' to be applied to Herrnhuter piety.[39] You know that I have two friends among the women there, whose lives are emphatically not perverted. On the contrary, their sensibility and intellectual awareness are as steady as their piety is deep."

Eduard responded, laughing. "My dear young lady," he said, "you will have to mark up Leonhardt's description to his lack of acquaintance. He only repeats what some people say, for you can be sure he has never looked into[40] a Herrnhuter establishment, unless it was to buy a good saddle or to examine some unusually fine material. At such a time he may have caught sight of the very comely children who live at the Sisters' Home, but that is about all.[41] As for me, I would definitely be mistaken if I were

36. In 1806: "to lose."

37. In 1806: "her almost audacious way."

38. In 1806: "put."

39. In 1806: "but at the very least I do not allow your fancy word 'perversion' to conjoin the two."

40. In 1806: "seen."

41. Ed. note: Schleiermacher knew the Sisters' Houses well. His sister Lotte, who was very close to him throughout his life, had entered the *Schwesternhaus* at Gnadenfrei in 1783, and he had visited her there several times. From ages fourteen to eighteen (1783–1787) he himself had attended Brethren schools in the Herrnhuter villages of Niesky and Barby. Nobility often sent their children to such colonies, to obtain a high-level classical education in the setting of intimate rural communal life. Hard work and frequent worship were the rule; but there was also much singing and instrumental music, in keeping with the basically

to admit to such a characterization as a general rule. Do bear with us a minute, however, and observe that we were speaking not[42] of the merits or characteristics of these different churches but only of Sophie; and so, if you take a good look at her, you must surely find[43] no suspicion of her connection with either. This is the case, for you know how these things are, and without panning your two friends, Karoline, you will admit that a girl who can satisfy her religious sense in the bosom of her family, and who has kept her innocence and simplicity, will not find the world terribly threatening, and that if she has been used to a free and happy life, it is unthinkable that she should shut herself up in a cloistered Sisters' Home, unless she has some strange quirk. Besides, as I was going to remark to Leonhardt, the same is true of people who go over to Rome or Herrnhut, except perchance under[44] special motivating circumstances of the sort you are defending. I mean, proselytes of either kind, so far as my experience goes, are not religiously inclined from childhood up as Sophie is. Rather, as the saying goes, it is the flirty women and the tricky politicians who in later life, or having suffered misfortune, go religious. Accordingly, these people, for the most part at least, are the kind whose former pursuits have been handled in an entirely external fashion,[45] whether in scholarship or in art

---

celebratory (if sometimes overly strict and maudlin) atmosphere of Brethren religion. The whole community was organized into "choirs," according to age and gender. Apart from their educational and missionary activities, these people (whose forefathers had immigrated from Moravia during the Thirty Years' War of 1618–1648) were also known for their fine handicrafts (*Handwerk*).

42. In 1806: "are speaking."
43. In 1806: "of Sophie, so you must surely find."
44. In 1806: "except under."
45. In 1806: "been pursued in an entirely worldly fashion."

or in the home,[46] the relation of these to higher things[47] having been completely overlooked. Now, when this relation begins to dawn on them somehow, they enter a new world, and they react to it[48] like little children. They reach out[49] for its glitter, whether this is reflected off the object of their attraction and magnified[50] or whether it derives from some inner fire and draws them less on account of its own flame than because the surroundings are so dark.[51] Thus we can say that in their penitence something of their sin ever remains, in that they tend[52] to throw the blame for their previous torpor and blindness upon the church they belonged to. They act as if the sacred fire had not been preserved within it, and as if nothing but a cold formalism of empty words and dry, outworn ceremony had been left in its stead."

"Your description may well be correct in some cases," replied Leonhardt; "but you have certainly not put your finger on the only source of this evil. It is also true that in many cases the tendency appears to arise from within, as with our little one here. It really is remarkable that I of all people, and others whom your circle calls unbelievers, should have to exhort you to beware of unbelief—though, of course, it is only disbelief in superstition[53] and all that relates to it that I am talking about. I do not need to assure you, Eduard, that I honor and admire the beauty of piety,[54] but it must be an internal thing and stay that way. If it would

46. *Häusliches Leben*; in 1806: *Ehe* ("marriage").

47. In 1806: "to the infinite."

48. In 1806: "somehow, they react to it."

49. In 1806: "children and reach out."

50. In 1806: "whether this is something externally magnified"

51. In 1806: "or an inner fire that draws them on account of the some other force and the darkness of its surroundings."

52. In 1806: "remains, namely in their tending."

53. *Unglaube an den Aberglauben*; in 1806: "it is disbelief."

54. *Frömmigkeit*; 1806: *Religiosität* ("religiousness").

move out so as to[55] mold the actual circumstances of life, this would lead to fossilizing separatism and spiritual pride[56] —the most detestable consequences one can imagine and the exact opposite of what piety ought properly to produce.[57] As you will recall, Eduard, when we discussed this subject only recently, we considered that the so-called spiritual[58] profession could escape danger from this direction only if the same piety expected of its members were extended over the entire body. Moreover, at the time you said that among the large number of clergy you know, by virtue of your office, you had trouble dredging up examples of even a couple of them who had not fallen into such evil. It is still more damaging, however, when the laity, who have no special calling to that profession, devote themselves to such unconventional piety. It strikes me as just like some kind of drunken delirium! Catholic practice that is taken up with purely external works of piety is simply another example of the same thing; and so is the practice of those among our own people who swarm about some narrow-minded, exclusive opinion.[59]

"Now, your little one, as it appears, has already taken a drink from the same cup, and not a slight one for such a child.[60]

55. In 1806: "when it would move out and."

56. In 1806: "lead to spiritual pride."

57. In 1806: "pride, which is in the end is no different from the most wayward and deranged superstition."

58. Ed. note: In German usage, the clergy are often referred to in this way (*Geistlicher*), then and still.

59. In 1806: "As you will recall, Eduard, only recently we discussed this subject, and among the so-called spiritual profession (*geistlichen Stande*), persons whom you indeed know from far and wide by virtue of your office, you had trouble dredging up examples of even a couple of them who had not been corrupted by it. Now, among the Catholics the laity too are involved in such delirium, through works of piety they perform that have nothing but an external value."

60. In 1806: "for a child."

If you are then going to be so foolish as to favor[61] her ambition to become a pious *Frau*, or even to nudge it along, where will it eventually lead her[62] but into a convent or to the Sisters? For the rest of us cannot manage such practices very well out in the world. Look at this playful devotion for the Christ child and her adoration of the halo that she herself made for him. Isn't this the most unmistakable germ of superstition? Isn't this sheer idolatry? Watch out, my dear friends. If you don't put a check to this behavior, her life is going to end up in something void of reason. Obviously, however, the evidence shows that what you are doing is very far from putting a check on it, for you are even exposing the child to the Bible. I would hope that you do not just give it over to her, to read as she likes. Yet, it is still the same thing if you read from it in her presence, or if her mother relates things to her from its pages. The mythical feature is bound to strike her imagination; and odd, distorted images[63] cannot help but arise that cannot find[64] common ground with sound concepts later on. A mere letter is then sanctified in her mind and enthroned; and the unrestrained caprice that leads the child on will attach to it absurdities it never contained. For that matter, the miraculous sheen[65] alone will breed superstition; and when a person gets that fragmented,[66] one is ripe for all manner of delusions—one's own brand of fanaticism[67]—and one is easily deceived by systems implanted from without.

61. In 1806: "to favor and nudge along."

62. In 1806: "where will it lead her."

63. In 1806: "odd images."

64. In 1806: "cannot take."

65. In 1806: "never contained; the miraculous sheen."

66. Ed. note: The 1806 noun changed into an adjective here was *Unzusammenhang*, the lack of a sense of order and interconnectedness.

67. *Schwärmerei*. Ed. note: At the time, for example, various brands of pietism such as that of the Herrnhuter Brethren, were widely accused of this falsely enthusiastic, irrational behavior. At that time, Halle was a

"Listen, at a time when even the preachers are laudably zealous in dispensing with the Bible as much as possible in the pulpit, to put these books back into the hands of children, for whom they were never intended anyway, is the worst thing you could do! It would be better for these books—to use their own words against them—if a millstone were fastened round their neck and if they were drowned in the depth of the sea than that they should give offense to the little ones.[68] Who knows what may happen if they take in the sacred story with their other fairy tales? Think what harm could arise if one's heart leaned upon such a faith, and if one's life were ordered by a faith that has no more truth in it than this! Consider especially how hazardous it would be for those of the other sex.[69] A boy will sooner help himself out of it and in good time find more solid ground. Or,[70] if things turn out for the worse, just let him study theology for a year, and that will cure him for sure!"

"Now," said Eduard after waiting to see whether the peroration was finished, "it behooves me to defend our Leonhardt here against those of you who do not yet know him well,[71] lest his speech appear more wicked than it was meant to be.[72] He is really not so deeply sunk into disbelief as might seem, and he has little in common with those Enlightenment thinkers[73] of ours with whom he associates himself. It is just that he has not yet entirely made up his mind on the matter; therefore, he continually mixes jesting and serious opinion—and in such a remarkable

primary crossroads of pietism and rationalism.

68. Matthew 18:6.

69. In 1806: "Whether the other fairy tales bear as much validity as that story does or as little, both are alike pernicious in their influence, especially for those of the other sex."

70. In 1806: "out of it. Or."

71. In 1806: "who do not know him."

72. In 1806: "than it was."

73. *Aufklärern* (or "rationalists").

way that not everyone can tell the two apart. Thus, if we were to take seriously everything that he says, he would assuredly be more than a little amused with us. So, I am going to restrict my remarks to your jesting, my dear friend. Regarding your serious views enough has been said already.

"Let me tell you a story, then, and please don't be too alarmed at it. It is true that the girl does hear a great deal straight from the Bible, including the notion that Joseph was only the foster father of Christ. What I want to tell you about happened a year ago or more. She had asked who his real father was, then. Her mother answered that he had no other father than God. To this she replied that she believed God to be her father too, but that she would not like on that account to be without me, and that maybe it already belonged to the sufferings of Christ that he had no real father, for it is a very wonderful thing to have one. Whereupon she snuggled up to me and fondled my hair, as children do. You can see from this what a penchant she already has for dogmatics, and how extraordinarily[74] predisposed she is toward becoming a martyr for the belief in conception by the virgin Mary![75] What is more, she really does take the sacred story in somewhat the aspect of a tale, for there are moments when the young girl wins the upper hand over the little child, when she has her doubts about certain factual details in the story and asks whether they are also to be understood literally.[76] As you can see, this is 'bad' enough, and she has come very close to the allegorical interpretation of some of the church fathers."

"Hearing you banter like this," said Karoline, "usually encourages me to put in my two cents' worth as well. I can join you in pointing out that she made the halo around the Christ child, and in defiance of all heathenly disposed artists at that! Indeed,

74. In 1806: "splendidly."

75. In 1806: "in the immaculate conception by Mary!"

76. In 1806: "are also so true in a literal sense."

she already frequently scrawls such sketches when she is at her reading and writing—thus already half without thinking, which is all the more 'badly' Catholic. But seriously, I think we are all the more secure from both extremes. Why? Because among the Herrnhuter Brethren, people do not think much of pictures; hence, she would find their life too unartistic for her taste. As for the Catholics, you are always saying that the best of those who have gone over from our church have done so because they could find a firm union of religion with the arts there, something that is lacking among us.[77] Since Sophie has already accomplished this union in her own way, she will feel no need to attach herself to that form of it which[78] often comes out so odd and tasteless."

"Well!" retorted Leonhardt. "If the young ladies are bent on tripping me up, I might as well go all the way! In my opinion, she is just as well off going Catholic with her applying the arts to religion, for I don't like that at all. As a Christian I am very unartistically inclined, and as an artist I am very unchristian. I don't like the straitlaced church that Schlegel has depicted for us in his also rather straitlaced[79] stanzas;[80] nor am I pleased with any

77. In 1806: "But seriously, I am now laughing at Leonhardt over his concern yet again, for on that score a basis for motivating is simply missing. Or did you not say, Leonhardt, that the best people go to that church because it would be in league with the arts?" Ed. note: In 1808, among the early Romantics, his friend and onetime housemate (in the late 1790s) Friedrich Schlegel (1772–1829) already long a lover of things medieval, converted to Catholicism. By 1805 Schlegel was already leaning in that direction. Schlegel's wife, Dorothea Veit Mendelssohn Schlegel (1763–1839), also converted to the Catholic Church in 1808.

78. In 1806: "to another form of it in which art."

79. In 1806: "in his straitlaced."

80. Ed. note: As I noted in the 1967 edition, the reference is to the poem "Der Bund der Kirche mit dent Künsten" (1800), in August Wilhelm Schlegel (1767–1845), *Sämmtliche Werke*, edited by Eduard Böcking, Bd. I (Leipzig, 1846), 87–96. See Patsch's lengthy quotation in KGA I/5 (1995), 59–62. Also prominent among the early Romantics in

poor frozen beggar's art that is satisfied to find shelter in it. If the arts are not to live eternally young and fertile and independent, forming their own world as everyone will agree ancient mythology did, I want no part in them. Likewise, religion as we think of it also strikes me as pretty weak and suspect when it wants to lean on the arts for support."

"Watch out, Leonhardt!" said Ernst. "Your critics may just throw your words back at you when you least want them! Have you not only recently pressed upon us your view that life and art are as little opposites as life and science, also that a truly cultured life would be a work of art, a production of beauty, the most unobstructed union of plastic and musical art? Now, they will contend that you do not really believe that life should be 'sheltered' by religion or be inspired by it, and that religion is therefore to have no existence except in words, where you occasionally need it for some reason or other."

"We are not going to say that," interposed Ernestine. "Furthermore," she said, "we have had enough of this idle controversy, which wearies the rest of us since we cannot share an unalloyed delight in disputation with you."[81]

"And we are obviously one," added Eduard, "if in nothing else then certainly in the feeling of goodwill,[82] which is so especially expressed in our life on this day. This is so, for what else is the lovely custom of exchanging gifts than a forthright way of showing our religious joy—a joy which expressed itself, as joy always does, in unsought kindliness or in giving or in serving? In this instance especially, the great gift in which we all rejoice together is reflected in our lesser gifts; and the more purely this whole mood stands out, the more strikingly is our sensibility affected by it. Moreover, it was on this account, dear Ernestine,

---

Germany, he was Friedrich Schlegel's older brother. Their father was a pastor, as was Schleiermacher's father.

81. In 1806: "in disputation."

82. In 1806: "added Eduard, 'in this lovely thought.'"

that we were so entranced with your arrangement of things this evening: You expressed our own sensibility regarding Christmas so aptly. We were young again, felt like children. We had the serene joy of living in the new world that we owe to the child we celebrate. All this lay in the glimmering light, in the greenery and blossoms scattered all about, and in our longing to see what was being readied for us."

"Yes, indeed," said Karoline, "what we feel in these days is such a pure, pious joy in Christmas itself! So much so that I was sorry to hear Ernst utter a little while ago that it could be enhanced by happy events or expectations in one's external life, though he probably wasn't completely serious in this claim. Anyway, as to[83] the significance of our little gifts, their value lies not in what they specifically refer to at all but quite generally in the fact that they refer to something. What is important is that we intend to give pleasure, and that we likewise show how distinctly our picturing of each dear friend is involved in what we give them. In my own feeling, at any rate, there is a very definite distinction between that higher, more generally focused joy and my liveliest participation in what may be confronting you all, my dear friends. Moreover, I would rather say just the opposite from what Ernst did: that the latter experience is enhanced by the former. If something fine or gratifying is presented to us at a time when we are most inwardly conscious of the greatest and finest thing of all, then that consciousness will be taken up into our awareness of it. Furthermore, in relation to the glorious salvation of the world, all love takes on a greater significance, as does everything good. You know, I still clearly[84] feel what has been very much a part of my own experience: I mean, even with the deepest pain this joy can blossom within us unhindered, can cleanse and soothe the pain without being destroyed by it. That

83. In 1806: "Anyway, what he said regarding."
84. In 1806: "strongly."

is how basic this joy is. That is how immediately rooted it is in an imperishable source."

"I agree," said Eduard. "According to the measure Ernst offered, today I could[85] easily be the least blessed among us, and yet I feel overflowing with the joy of pure serenity, which I think could of a surety withstand anything that might happen to me.[86] It is a mood in which I could challenge fate—or, if that sounds arrogant, a mood in which I could at least stand up to any challenge; and such composure is indeed[87] to be desired for everyone. A full consciousness of this mood, however, and an apt appreciation of it, I feel I owe in part to the fact that our little one has invited us to express it in music, for every fine feeling comes completely to the fore only when we have found the right musical expression for it. Not the spoken word, for this can never be anything but indirect—a plastic element, if I may put it that way—but a real, uncluttered tone. Furthermore, it is precisely to religious feeling that music is most closely related. There is much talk about how we might restore a common expression of religious feeling today; but scarcely anyone has considered that by far the best results might be achieved if we were, once again, to grant singing a more proper relation to the spoken word. What the word has declared the tones of music must make alive, in harmony conveying it to one's whole inner being and holding it fast there."

"Doubtless no one will deny," Ernst added, "that music attains its perfection only in the religious sphere. Comic music, which exists only by way of pure contrast, rather confirms than refutes this point. A serious opera, on the other hand,[88] could scarcely be composed without some religious basis—and the

85. In 1806: "offered, I could."
86. In 1806: "which could of a surety withstand anything."
87. In 1806: "and such is surely."
88. In 1806: "An opera."

same would hold for all other elevated words of musical art, for no one can discover the true spirit of the art in its derivative, artificially crafted forms."

"This rather close affinity," Eduard went on, "probably lies in the fact that only in immediate relation to the highest in our lives—to religion, and to some distinct form of it—does music have enough concrete reference, without being tied to some mere contingency, to be intelligible. Christianity is a unique theme presented in endless variations. Yet, these variations are also conjoined by a single law intrinsic to each, which gives them a distinct character overall. I also think it is true what someone has said, that we can well dispense with particular words in church music but not with the singing itself.[89] A miserere, a gloria, or a requiem: what special words are required for these? Their very character conveys plenty of meaning and suffers no essential change even though accompanying words may be replaced with others, so long as these are singable and fit the timing of the music; and this is true no matter what the language.[90]

89. Ed. note: Schleiermacher includes himself in this reference. With two changes, noted here, the following passage from discourse IV of his work *On Religion* was included in all three editions (1799, 1806, 1821): "The intimate relation between the muse of harmony and religion still [1806 adds: "almost"] belongs to the mysteries. From of yore that muse had laid upon the altars of religion the most glorious and consummate works of her most devoted students. In sacred hymns and chorales, to which the words of poets are only loosely and airily appended, there are breathed such things as precise speech is powerless to grasp. In such instances the tones of thought and sense intermingle and support each other until all is full of the holy, full of the infinite, and can be filled no more." In 1821 the segment "still belongs to the mysteries. From of yore" was replaced by "has long been known and interpreted, though recognized only be a few. From of old." This translation is from my presentation of all three editions (forthcoming from Cascade Books).

90. In 1806: "plenty of meaning" (the rest is added in 1826).

Indeed,[91] no one would say that anything of gross importance[92] was lost even if one didn't get the words at all.[93] For this reason Christianity and music must adhere closely together, because they elevate and give radiance to each other. As Jesus was welcomed by the choir of angels, so we[94] accompany him on his way with the sound of instruments and singing, on through to the great hallelujah of the ascension. And music such as Handel's *Messiah* is, for me, like a sweeping proclamation of Christianity as a whole."[95]

"Yes," agreed Friederike,[96] "it is the most religious note that penetrates into the heart most surely."

"And it is a singing piety," nodded[97] Karoline, "which ascends most gloriously and directly to heaven. Nothing peculiar or accidental restrains either. What Eduard has said reminds me of something I have read not long ago, and you will guess right away from whom it comes. The words ran something like this: Never does music weep or laugh over particular circumstances, but always over life itself."

91. In 1806: "and."

92. In 1806: "of importance."

93. In 1806: "get the words."

94. In 1806: "Jesus was welcomed by the choir of angels, and we" Ed. note: See Luke 2:13–14.

95. Ed. note: This sentence was added in 1826. *Messiah* was first performed in 1741. The *Singakademie* (Choral Society) in Berlin, in which Schleiemacher regularly sang tenor over the last twenty-five years of his life, first performed it on Good Friday, April 5, 1822, and often thereafter. Just above, reference is no doubt made to the concluding chorus (whose two parts are known separately as "Worthy Is the Lamb" and "Amen") and to an earlier chorus commonly called the Hallelujah Chorus. He may have heard it elsewhere before 1822, for it had been introduced into Germany at Hamburg in 1772, as Patsch has indicated (KGA I/5, 65n).

96. In 1806: "'Yes,' said Friederike, 'in general.'"

97. In 1806: "added."

"We will want to add, in the name of Jean Paul,"[98] said Eduard, "that particular events are[99] only the passing notes for music. Its true content is the great chords of our mind and heart,[100] which marvelously and with the most varied voices ever resolve themselves into the same harmony, in which only the major and minor keys are to be distinguished, only the masculine and the feminine."

"See," Agnes broke in, "now we're back again to what I was saying. How much can what is strictly personal or particular—whether we speak of present or future, joy or sorrow—give to a mind and heart stirred in the moods of piety, or take from it? As little as the passing notes, leaving only a faint trace behind them, can disturb the harmonious flow of music."

"Listen, Eduard," Leonhardt suddenly interjected, "this repose[101] of yours just seems to me too awful for words. It completely denies the facts of life, and[102] I must enter a complaint against you for that. How can you bear it," he went on with lowered voice, "to have Agnes talk like this[103] —she who lives in the most beautiful and blessed expectation of all?"

"And why not?" she herself replied. "Isn't the purely personal also something left behind in this area too? Think now:

98. Ed. note: Karoline was referring to *Jean Paul*, the popular name of the contemporary poet Johann Paul Freidrich Richter (1763–1825), whose three volumes of reflections on aesthetics had appeared in the previous year (*Vorschule der Aesthetik,* Hamburg, 1804). His writings are still valued in Germany for their humor and educative interest. Patsch (KGA I/5, 65n) found Karoline's allusion in *Flegeljahre: Eine Biographie von Jean Paul Richter*, Bd. 2 (Tübingen, 1804), S. 110; also in his *Sämtliche Werke* I/10 (Weimar, 1934), 171.

99. In 1807: "were."

100. *Gemüth.*

101. In 1806: "this repose and surrender."

102. In 1806: "for words, and."

103. In 1806: "say this."

isn't the newborn child subject to the greatest dangers? And look how easily an unsteady flame can be snuffed out even by the slightest draft. A mother's love, however, is what is eternal in us; it is the fundamental chord of our being."

"And so you are indifferent, then," queried Leonhardt, "as to whether you can cultivate what you would like for your child, or whether it may be torn from you in the first helpless stage of life?"

"Indifferent? Who would say that?" she retorted. "To the contrary, the inner life, the status of one's soul, is not destroyed thereby. Do you believe, then, that love is directed to what a child can be formed into? What can we form, actually? No, love is directed toward what we believe to be lovely and divine in the child already, as soon as its soul begins to find expression."

"You see," said Ernestine, "in this sense every mother is another Mary. Every mother has a child divine and eternal, and every mother devoutly looks out for the stirrings of the higher spirit within that child. Into such a love, moreover, no fate can bring ruinous affliction; nor do the pernicious weeds of maternal vanity spring up to choke it. An old Simeon may prophesy that a sword will pierce through her soul; Mary[104] but ponders such words in her heart. The angels may rejoice, and the wise men come and worship; yet she does not exalt herself but continues in the same devout and humble love."[105]

---

104. In 1806: "she."

105. Ed. note: See Luke 1:26–35; 2:19, 25–36; and Matthew 2:1–12. Among Schleiermacher's Christmas sermons, see those for Luke 1:31–32 (1821); 2:15–20 (1802, 1831); and 2:25–32 (1791). That for Matthew 2:1–12 was preached on Epiphany Sunday, January 7, 1821. See Terrence N. Tice, *Schleiermacher's Sermons* (Lewiston, NY: Mellen, 1997), # 188d (1) for the latter sermon. Epiphany was not especially celebrated in the Prussian Reformed churches in Schleiermacher's time. The only other sermon he preached on that day (January 6, 1833) falls within a series of sermons on Mark.

"If you women were not clever at expressing everything so charmingly[106] that one cannot wish to infringe upon what you say," piped up Leonhardt, "one might find[107] much to say against it. If all that you contend really stood up, unquestionably you would be the heroines of this age—you precious, idealistic mistresses of *Schwärmerei*,[108] with your contempt for the actual and particular—and one should have to regret that your congregation is not stronger, and that you lack able-bodied sons ready to bear arms and do battle for you. You should be the true Christian ladies of Sparta! Therefore, look to your words, and hold to what you have promised;[109] for there may be hard trials before you, in which you are forced to make them good.[110] The situation is already upon us. Great forces of destiny are stomping about our neighborhood, with steps that make the earth tremble; and we know not how they may draw us in. Would that our present actuality may not take revenge, by its arrogant, overwhelming power, on your humble contempt!"

"My good friend," responded Ernst, "the women will scarcely be inferior to us in this regard; and, in fact, the whole time of testing that is upon us does not seem to me much their affair.[111] From a distance, the prospect of domestic misery ap-

---

106. In 1806: "If everything were not expressed so charmingly by you women."

107. In 1806: "there would be."

108. *Schwärmerinen*: "women enthusiasts." Ed. note: Leonhardt finds pietistic *Schwärmerei* distasteful in every form.

109. In 1806: "However, if your claims do not stand up, look out!"

110. In 1806: "to stand the test."

111. In 1806: "does not seem to me very great." Ed. note: This work appeared in January 1806. In October, Napoleon's troops occupied Halle, in anticipation and response to which Schleiermacher, as university preacher, delivered a brief series of "sociopolitical" sermons that came to be famous, especially: (1) "How Greatly the Dignity of a Person is Enhanced when one Adheres with All one's Soul to the Civil Union to

pears to loom large, but as it draws near, the picture begins to fall into its many components. The once-apparent impact[112] crumbles; and all that is left turns out to be only[113] these bits and pieces, their force confronted[114] by the comparable force of things already familiar to us. What must concern us men[115] in these matters is nothing the importance of which hangs on distance or proximity, but precisely that which does not fall directly within the women's sphere[116] but can arouse them only through us and on our account."

---

which One Belongs" (Aug. 24, 1806); (2) "The Greater Dignity of Those Who must Adhere to a Particular Association," an outline for Aug. 24; (3) "That, Overall, Peace Resides in the Reign of God," Oct. 12, 1806; (4) "Where God Holds Sway There Must Be Peace," an outline for Oct. 12; (5) "On Making Use of Public Disasters," Nov. 23, 1806; "That Recent Times are No Worse Than Earlier Times," Dec. 28, 1806; and (6) "What We Are and Are Not to Fear," Jan. 1, 1807. See *Schleiermacher's Sermons* (1997), # 76c (4–7, 4a–5a) and #77c.

112. In 1806: "the once large image."

113. In 1806: "that is left is ever simply."

114. In 1806: "mitigated."

115. In 1806: "us."

116. The phrase that follows was added in 1826.

3

Christmas Stories

In the meantime Sophie had been mostly at the piano getting acquainted with her newly acquired treasures. Part of them she did not know, and many of those she knew she wanted to greet at once as her own possessions. At this moment she could be heard singing a chorale from a cantata, her voice carrying with particular clarity the lines:

> Who gave his Son that we might ever live,
> All things to us with him shall he not give?[1]

Upon which there followed the magnificent fugue:

> If I possess but thee, I ask no more of earth or heaven.[2]

When she had finished, she closed the keyboard and returned to the drawing room.

"Look there," exclaimed Leonhardt, when he spied her coming—"our little prophetess! Now I shall determine how far she is still under your influence." Stretching out his hand to her, he asked: "Tell me, little one, wouldn't you rather be merry than sad?"

"I do not think I am either at just this moment," she replied.

---

1. Ed. note: cf. Romans 8:32.
2. Ed. note: cf. Psalm 13:25.

"What! Not merry after receiving so many lovely presents? Ah, the solemn music must have made you feel that way! But you have not quite understood what I meant. What I asked, no doubt unnecessarily, was which of the two you would rather be: merry or sad?"

"Oh, that's hard to say," she responded. "I do not particularly favor one or the other. I always just like to be whatever I am at the moment."

"Now you've got me puzzled all over again, my little sphinx. What do you mean by that?"

"Well," she said, "all I know[3] is that sometimes feelings of gladness and sorrow get strangely mixed up and fight each other; and that makes me uneasy, because I can tell,[4] as Mother has also pointed out, that something is always wrong or out of kilter then, and so I don't like it."

"All right," he asked again, "suppose you have only one feeling or the other, is it all the same to you whether you are merry or sad?"

"Why no! Each time I just like to be what I am, and what I like to be is not a matter of indifference to me. Oh, Mother," she went on, turning to Ernestine, "please help! He is questioning me in such a strange way, and I can't at all get to an understanding of[5] what he is getting at. Let him ask the grownups, for they will certainly know better how to answer him."[6]

---

3. In 1806: "understand."

4. In 1806: "each other and then I feel very well."

5. In 1806: "and I don't understand at all."

6. In 1806: "will certainly understand him better." Ed. note: At least as early as 1792, when he reached the age of 24, Schleiermacher was expressing a disposition and considered viewpoint close that of Sophie. According to this view, articulated then in his essay *On What Gives Value to Life*, in themselves so-called happiness and good fortune are not at any time the supreme ends of life, but what brings lasting value is being able to accept whatever comes with an open disposition and

"Actually," said Ernestine, "I don't think you will get much further with her, Leonhardt. She isn't at all accustomed to sorting out her experiences."

Ernst was smiling at him broadly. "But don't let this one attempt scare you off," he comforted. "Catechizing is nonetheless a fine art, of which one can make as good use in the courts as elsewhere. Also, one always learns something from it, unless of course one has started off on the wrong track!"

"But isn't she going to have any feeling about this?" Leonhardt asked of Ernestine, ignoring Ernst's jesting. "I mean, doesn't she know whether she would prefer a glad state of mind to a sad one?"

"Who knows?" she rejoined. "What do you think, Sophie?"

"I really don't know, Mother. I can be satisfied in one attitude or the other, and just now I was feeling[7] extraordinarily fine without being in either one. Only he makes me uneasy with his questions,[8] because I do not know how to arrange[9] all that I

---

a well-informed ability to act appropriately. This essay was translated, with introduction and notes, by Edwina Lawler and Terrence N. Tice (Schleiermacher: Studies and Translations 14, Lewiston, NY: Mellen, 1995). The approach, basically calm and celebratory and as far from any stoic resignation as Sophie's was, remained steady throughout his life and was frequently indicated in his philosophical ethics, sermons, and theological writings. From 1794 on, the key component of self-development (trying continually to learn from experience to serve one's own growth) was added. From even earlier on, he also folded in the component of trying to understand and know the world—eventually nature viewed as an interconnected whole—including the communal life of human beings and their culture. For other sustained insights that had arisen by 1796, see Tice, *Schleiermacher*, Abingdon Pillars of Theology (Nashville: Abingdon, 2006).

7. In 1806: "and at present I feel."

8. In 1806: "only his questions make me uneasy."

9. In 1806: "can't withstand."

am supposed to pull together to answer them." Thereupon she softly kissed her mother's hand and retreated to the far end of the room, now dark but for the lingering glow of a few lamps, to seek the company of her Christmas presents.

"Well, this she has clearly shown us," uttered Karoline only half aloud, "what that childlike sensibility[10] is without which one cannot enter into the reign of God. It is simply to accept each mood and feeling for itself and to desire only to have them pure and whole."

"True," spoke Eduard, "except that she is no longer just a child, but a young girl; and thus this is not altogether the sensibility of a child."

Karoline looked over at him and went on: "What you say is true enough, but only from our point of view. Think of the complaints one hears from both young and old, even in these special days of childlike celebration,[11] that they can no longer enjoy themselves so much as when they were children. I would just say that these complaints surely do not arise from people who have had such a happy childhood. Only yesterday I was saying that my capacity for lively enjoyment is as great as ever it was, in fact greater. The people who heard this were astonished, and I could only marvel that they were!"

"Yes," joked Leonhardt, "and the poor child herself will often be thought silly by such ogres as these, even when she has done nothing more than react with childlike joy over something requiring girlish dignity! Let it pass, though, my fine child, for these gainsayers are so deprived that nature has assigned them a second childhood at life's end, so that when they have reached this goal they may take one last consoling draught from the cup of joy, to close their long, doleful, dreary years."

"Surely this matter is more serious and tragic than funny," countered Ernst. "For me, at least, scarcely anything makes me

10. *Kindersinn.*
11. *Kinderfreude.*

shudder more than the vision you have just stirred up. How horrible that the great body of humankind should become unaware of the beautiful growth of a human life, and be tormented with boredom, simply because they have to leave the first objects of childish delight behind but never nourish the capacity for gaining higher things! I do not know whether to say they even look upon life, or are even in attendance, for even to do this[12] would seem to be too much for their utter incapacity to bear. In this way would their life go on, until at last, out of nothing, a second childhood would be born. Yet, such a childhood is as much related to the first as a contrary old dwarf is to a lovely and winsome child, or as the wavering flicker of a dying flame is to the embracing splendor and dancing form of one newly lit."

"One thing leads me to enter an objection," spoke up Agnes. "Is it true that our[13] first objects of delight as children have to be dropped behind before we can attain to higher things? May there not be a way of attaining these higher things without letting the first go? Does life begin, then, with a sheer illusion, in which there is no truth at all, nothing enduring? I wonder how I am to understand this quandary.[14] Think of the person who has achieved a mature awareness of self and of the world, and who has found God. Obviously this does not happen without struggle and conflict. Do this person's joys, then, depend on[15] destroying not only what is evil in one's life but also what is innocent and faultless? This is indeed how we always designate what is childlike—or, if you prefer, even what is childish. Or must time already have killed off, by I don't know what poison, the pristine

12. In 1806: "all this."
13. In 1806: "Do our."
14. In 1806: "what is your honest opinion about this quandary?"
15. In 1806: "Does this begin with."

joys of life? Moreover, must the transition out of the one state into the other pass, in every instance,[16] through a 'nothing'?"

"One might indeed call it a nothing," added Ernestine thoughtfully. "And yet it seems that men, in contrast to women, tend to lead an odd, wild sort of life between childhood and their better days, a life passionate and perplexed. They will admit this themselves—one might almost say the best men will admit it most of all. On the one hand, the period[17] looks like a continuation of childhood, the delights of which also have their own impetuous and disruptive character. On the other hand, the period takes the form of[18] a restless striving, an indecisive, ever-changing grasping and letting go that we women are simply unable to understand. In our gender, the two tendencies also fuse, but less perceptibly.[19] The course of our entire life already lies indicated in our childhood play, except that as we grow older the higher meaning of this and that gradually becomes clear.[20] Even when, in our own way, we come to an understanding of God and of the world, we tend to express our sublimest, tenderest feelings over and over again in those same precious trifles and with that same gentle demeanor that put us on friendly terms with the world in our childhood days."[21]

"Thus," said Eduard, "we see that in the development of their spiritual nature—though it must be the same in both, men and women do have their different ways—to the end that here too they may become one by sharing what they know with each other. It may well be true, and it seems clearly so to me, that

16. In 1806: "over and over again."

17. In 1806: "most of all. The period."

18. In 1806: "character. Yet, in this period there is also."

19. In 1806: "The two tendencies also fuse among us, but imperceptibly."

20. In 1806: "in each of us the higher meaning of this gradually becomes clearer."

21. In 1806: "that initially put us on friendly terms with the world."

the contrast between the spontaneous and the reflective emerges more strongly in us men.[22] Moreover, during the period of transition it reveals itself in that restless striving, that passionate conflict with the world and within oneself that you referred to. In contrast, within the calm, graceful nature of women comes to light the continuity and inner unity of the two, the spontaneous and the reflective. With you, holy earnestness and blithesome play are everywhere effortlessly united."

"But then," Leonhardt jocularly countered, "we men, oddly enough, would be more Christian than the women! This would be so, for Christianity is always speaking of a conversion, a change of heart, a new life whereby 'the old man' is driven out, and of this, if what we have just heard is true, you women—leaving out a few Magdalenes—would have no need whatsoever."

"Still, Christ himself," rejoined Karoline, "was not converted. For this very reason he has always been the patron and protector of women; and whereas you men have only contended about him, we have loved and honored him. Or consider: What can you say against the notion that we have at last applied the correct interpretation to the old proverb that we women go right on being children while you men must first be turned about to become so again?"

"Furthermore, to bring this matter close to home," added Eduard: "what is the celebration of Jesus's infancy but the distinct acknowledgment of the immediate union of the divine with the being of a child, by virtue of which no conversion is further needed? Remember too the view that Agnes has expressed on behalf of all women. She said, in effect, that from the point of birth on they already presuppose and seek for the divine presence in their children, even as the church presupposes and seeks for it in Christ."

22. In 1806: "in us."

"Yes, this very festival," said Friederike, "is the most direct proof, and the best, that our situation really is as Ernestine has described it."

"How so?" asked Leonhardt.

"Because here," she replied, "one can examine the nature of our joy in small yet neither forgotten nor unrecognizable sections of our life story, to see whether this joy has undergone any number of sudden changes. One scarcely need put the question to our conscience, for the matter speaks for itself. It is obvious enough that on the whole women and girls are the soul of these little celebrations. They fuss the most over them, but they are also the most purely receptive, and they get the most heightened enjoyment. If these were left only to you men, they would soon go under. Through us alone do they become ongoing traditions.

"Yet, couldn't we also have religious joy for its own sake alone?"[23] she inquired. "And wouldn't that be so if we had made a new discovery of it only later on? So one may ask. For us, however, everything fits together now,[24] just as it did in our earlier years. Already in our childhood we attributed special significance to these gifts, for example. They meant more to us than the same gifts at other times. Then, of course, it was only a dim, mysterious presentiment of what has since gradually become clearer. Yet, we always most prefer it to appear in much the same shape as before. We will not let the accustomed symbol go. In fact, given the exactness with which the precious little moments of life stick in our memory, I think one could trace out, step by step, just how the higher awareness has emerged in us."

"Truly," said Leonhardt, "were it vividly and nicely done, as you can do it, we should have a fine series of vignettes if you would describe your Christmas joys to us, with all their most remarkable traits, and even a person who could not particu-

---

23. In 1806: "by itself?"
24. In 1806: "may ask. Still, everything does fit together."

larly share their immediate aim would still take delight in the telling."

"How politely he informs[25] us that it would bore him!" cried Karoline.

Ernestine said: "Admittedly, it might seem relatively unimportant both for those who have more appreciation for the subject and for those who would put up with it in gallant deference to the women's interests. Still," she went on, "let whoever has something interesting to tell along the lines of our conversation do so. To start off, I'll relate a relevant incident from my own childhood, even though some of you perhaps already know of[26] it. The other women can go on from where I leave off."

Friederike rose to her feet, remarking: "You know that I am not much good at relating stories. However, I should like to do something else that may give you pleasure. I will station myself at the piano and improvise on your narratives. In this way you can also hear something from me with your finer, heightened ear for music."

Ernestine

Ernestine commenced her account:

"All sorts of troubles had plagued the house I speak of prior to the Christmas season, and only shortly before had they reached their rather happy resolution. Hence, less had been done for the enjoyment of the children that was customary, and with far less care and industry. This provided a favorable occasion for satisfying a wish that I had already expressed, in vain, the year before. In those days, the so-called Christmas matins were held in the late-evening hours. These continued until about midnight, the songs alternating with discourses before an ever-changing and not particularly reverent assembly. With some hesitation,

25. In 1806: "tells."

26. In 1806: "should perhaps already be acquainted with it."

my parents finally allowed me to go, accompanied by my mother's chambermaid.

"I cannot easily recall any other Christmas[27] with such mild weather as there was that year. The heavens were swept of clouds, yet the evenings were almost warm. We walked in the neighborhood of the Christmas market, by now nearly over. Great bands of boys roamed about sporting the last cut-rate pipes, whistling birds, and humming tops, yelling as they ran here and there along the walks to the various churches. Only when we had come close by could we hear the organ, joined by the uneven voices of a few children and adults. Notwithstanding the seeming abundance of lamps and candles, the old, gray walls and pillars remained impervious to light, and only with effort could I make out a few isolated figures within. Nothing there to quicken delight! Still less could the quavering tones of the minister entice me to enter in. Quite disappointed, I was about to ask my companion to take me home and was taking one last look around when my eye caught something. It was a lady sitting in an open pew just under a lovely old monument, holding a small child to her bosom. Apparently giving little heed to the preacher, the singing, or anything else about her, she seemed to be sunk deep in her own thoughts, and her eyes were fixed upon the child. Irresistibly, I was drawn toward them, and my companion was obliged to follow as I moved closer. There, at that moment, I had suddenly come upon the sanctuary, the holy place, I had been seeking so long in vain.

"I stood before the noblest scene I had ever witnessed. The woman was simply dressed. Her grand and *gentil*[28] bearing made the open bench into an enclosed chapel. No one was sitting nearby, and yet she seemed not to have noticed my movements, even though I then stood directly before her. Her countenance seemed to display gladness in one moment, dejection in the

27. In 1806: "any other instance of this season."

28. The closest English word to the French *gentil* is "genteel."

next—her breath now trembling with joy, then holding the sighs of contentment back. Yet what was communicated through it all was a sense of affable serenity and of loving devotion, radiating gloriously from her dark, downcast eyes, which would have been completely hidden from me had I been any taller. The child also seemed to me uncommonly lovely. It stirred energetically and yet quietly, and it seemed to be absorbed in a half-unconscious dialogue of love and yearning with its mother.

"It was as if I were viewing an artist's picture of Mary and child in living exemplar. I was so deeply entranced that almost involuntarily I tugged at the woman's dress and asked, in a moved and pleading voice: 'May I give something to the sweet child?' Whereupon I emptied several handfuls of dainties, which I had brought along as provisions, upon his garments. The lady looked at me narrowly for a moment, then kindly drew me to her. She kissed my forehead and said: 'Yes, of course, dear little girl—today everyone is giving, and all for the sake of a child.'

"I kissed the hand she lightly placed about my neck and an outstretched hand of the tiny child, and I was quickly turning to leave when she said: 'Wait, I want to give something to you; perhaps I will recognize you by it when I see you again.' She searched about and drew from her hair a golden pin, set with a green stone, and she fastened this pin to my cloak. A second time I kissed her, lightly on her sleeve, and quickly left the church, brimming over with bliss.

"As I later learned, it was Eduard's oldest sister, that[29] glorious, tragic figure, who has influenced my life and my inner being more than anyone in this world. She soon became the guide and friend of my youth, and although I have had nothing but sorrows to share with her, yet I count my association with her among the loveliest, weightiest moments of my life. Eduard also stood behind her then, still a growing boy, though without my noticing him."

29. In 1806: "the."

Friederike appeared already to have known the story, so aptly did her playing accompany its graceful telling. Each part was made to harmonize with the total impression given. As Ernestine finished, she quietly modulated into a lovely hymn. Sophie, recognizing it at once, darted over to join in, and together they sang the beautiful verses of Novalis:[30]

> I see thee in a thousand forms,
> O Mary, lovingly expressed;
> Yet none can show thy deeper charms
> That move the soul within my breast.
>
> I only know the world's uproar
> Appears now as a vanished dream;
> And joys of Heaven, unknown before,
> Through all my heart for ever stream.

"Mother," observed Sophie as she returned to her place, "all that you have told me about Aunt Kornelie and the handsome young man I once met comes back to me vividly just now[31]— how he died so heroically, and so senselessly, for the cause of freedom. May I go get the pictures? We all know them very well, but I think this is a moment when we should look at them again."

---

30. Ed. note: From the famous *Spiritual Songs* of the German Romantic poet, Novalis (pen name for Friedrich von Hardenberg [1772–1801]). The translation is taken from W. Hastie's 1890 edition of the dialogue, 40. For the complete original, see *Novalis Werke, Briefe, Dokumente,* edited by Ewald Wasmuth, Bd. 1: *Die Dichtungen* (Heidelberg: Schneider, 1953), 436; or *Novalis Schriften,* edited by Jakob Minor, Bd. 1 (Jena: Diederichs, 1907), 86. The songs had also been published posthumously in Novalis's *Schriften*, edited by Friedrich Schlegel and Ludwig Tieck, 2. Th. (Berlin: Buchhandlung der Realschule 1802), 157–58. Cf. note 51 below.

31. In 1806: "vividly now."

Her mother nodded approval, and the child fetched two unframed pictures, products of Ernestine's brush. Both represented her friend and the son of her sorrow. The one showed him returning from battle, wounded but covered with glory. The other depicted how he took leave of her, thence to fall as one of the last sacrifices to that most bloodthirsty time.

The remembrances were painful and could be vented in only a few mournful words. Leonhardt deftly broke through them by asking Agnes: "Tell us about something else, child, to free us from the piercing pain, which belongs not at all to our feeling of celebration, as[32] in the same breath you might release us from the morbid worship of Mary into which these two have now sung us!"

Agnes

"All right, then," replied Agnes. "What I have to relate is rather less weighty, but perhaps that will be made up for by its gayer note. A year ago, as you know, we were all scattered during the Christmas season. I had already spent several weeks at my brother's, helping Luise with her first baby. The holy eve had begun there too, as is our own custom, with the assembling of male and female friends. To be sure, Luise[33] was fully recovered, but[34] I insisted on doing all the arrangements, and so I was overjoyed that the sheer contentment[35] and freshly aroused caring that everywhere pervades among people of goodwill on this festive day also prevailed there. Moreover, as this mood is naturally expressed with gifts and tokens of gladness and is garbed in joviality and free, childlike amusement, so it was among us.

---

32. In 1806: "and."

33. *Freunden und Freundinnen.* In 1806: "friends. Luise."

34. In 1806: "nevertheless."

35. In 1806: "and so the contentment."

"Suddenly, the nurse appeared in the room, carrying the wee infant. She went peering about the tables, and several times lightly exclaimed, in an almost plaintive voice: 'Has no one, then, provided for the babe? Have they completely forgotten him, then?' We soon gathered round the tiny, delicate creature, and voices rose, in earnest or in jest, saying that for all our love we could not give him joy, and how proper it was to have entrusted everything that pertained to him to his mother. Then the nurse was shown all these presents, which were also held up to the little one—dainty caps and stockings, suits, baby bibs, and spoons. Yet, neither the shine and clink of the fine metal, nor the dazzling or diaphanous white of the material seemed to rouse his senses. 'See, children!' I said to the others: 'He is still completely oriented toward his mother, and as yet even she can arouse in him only the ordinary feeling of satisfaction. His consciousness[36] is still united with hers; it dwells in her, and only in her can we cherish and gladden it.'

"'Even so, we have all been very narrow,' interjected one of the girls, 'in having thought only of the present moment like this. Doesn't the whole life of the child stand before its mother?' With these words she asked me for the keys, and several others hastened away, with the promise that they would be back soon. Ferdinand told them to hurry, for he also had something special in mind for the little one.

'Can you guess what I'm going to do?' he said to those who remained. 'I'm going to baptize him. I know no finer moment for it than this. Make the necessary preparations, and I'll be back by the time our friends return.'

"As quickly as possible, we dressed the child[37] in the most elegant of the clothes given him, and we had scarcely finished when the dispersed company returned with all sorts of gifts in hand. Jest and earnestness were wonderfully conjoined in them,

36. In 1806: "feeling."
37. In 1806: "dressed him."

as cannot be otherwise in any attempt to anticipate the future. There was material for making clothes—not only for his boyhood but for his wedding day too! A toothpick and a watch chain were presented, with the wish that it might be said of him in a better sense than of Churchill that 'when he plays with his watch chain or picks at his teeth out comes a poem'![38] There were also some elegant notepaper for writing his first love letter, some elementary textbooks in all sorts of languages and subjects, and a Bible, which was to be handed him on the occasion of his first instruction in the Christian faith. Indeed, his uncle, who is fond of making caricatures, even brought the prime requisite of 'a future dandy,' as he put it after Campe,[39] a pair of spectacles! And he would not rest until they were placed over the bright blue eyes of the babe. This brought on much laughter and joking; but Luise asserted, quite seriously, that with the exception of the spectacles—for he must surely have her and Ferdinand's good eyesight—she saw him now very vividly before her, yes quite prophetically, with his own distinct form and features in all the times and circumstances to which the gifts pointed. They teased her in vain about how old-fashioned he would probably

38. Ed. note: Charles Churchill (1731–1764) was an English literary and political satirist who suddenly rose to fame with his *Roseciad* (a poetic satire) and *Apology*, both published in 1761. I have searched in vain for the source of this remark, but it is quite in keeping with other remarks directed toward this prolific young writer at the time. As Patsch notes, Schleiermacher wrote to his close friend Henrietta Herz on 17 January 1806: "I would almost have marveled that you had not acquainted me with Churchill earlier" (*Aus Schleiermachers Leben: in Briefen*, Band II, 2.A. (Berlin: Reimer, 1860], 50).

39. *Auf Campisch.* In 1806: *Kampisch.* Ed. note: The unusual *Campisch* expression *Zierbold* that Schleiermacher mentions here refers to a dictionary published in 1801 by Joachim Heinrich Campe (1746–1818). It was devoted to an explanation and Germanizing of foreign expressions. See Patsch, KGA I/5 (1995), S. 76n, for more information on this word.

turn out to be if he should really honor each present by using it. The paper, especially, must be kept from yellowing!

"In the end we praised the person who gave the Bible, above all, for that he would most surely be able to use. I drew attention to the baby's attire, but no one suspected anything.[40] They thought only that this was a right, honorable manner of receiving their gifts. Hence they were all not a little surprised when Ferdinand entered, in full clerical dress, and the makeshift font was brought in.

"'Don't be too surprised, my friends,' he said. 'Agnes's earlier remark very naturally gave rise to the thought of baptizing the boy tonight. You shall all be witnesses, and by taking part you shall testify anew to your concern for his life as his friends.'[41] He halted, and looked at each one as their enthusiasm rose in response to his proposal. Then he went on: 'You have borne him gifts, gifts that point to a life of which he as yet knows nothing, just as gifts were also brought[42] before Christ that pointed to a glory of which the infant was as yet unaware. Let us, then, appropriate to him the finest gift of all, Christ himself, though in this moment it cannot yet accord him either joy or pleasure. For his sake, the power of the higher life,[43] which cannot yet exist in himself,[44] dwells not alone in his mother or in me but in us all. Moreover, as time goes on, this power must stream out to him from us all so that he may take it unto himself.'[45]

"And so, he gathered us about him and almost straightway passed from conversation into the sacred ceremony. With only slight allusion to the words 'Can anyone forbid that these be

40. In 1806: "but no one suspected any special occasion."

41. *Als theilnehmende Freunde seines lebens.*

42. In 1806: "were brought."

43. In 1806: "his religious feeling."

44. In 1806: "in him."

45. In 1806: "he must appropriate this power from us all."

baptized?'[46] he went on to speak of how the fact that a Christian child is welcomed with love and joy, and ever remains embraced by them, furnishes a guarantee that the Spirit of God will dwell in that child; of how the birthday celebration of the new world must be a day of love and joy; and of how the union of both is appropriately ordained for the initiation of a child of love also into the higher birth of godly life. As we all then laid hands upon the child, according to the fine old custom of that area, it was as if the rays of heavenly love and joy[47] converged upon the head and heart of the child in a new focus, and it was certainly our common feeling that they kindled a new life there, and that they would radiate out again in every direction."

"And so we have the same thing all over again," Leonhardt broke in, "only now it is a reversed-negative of a Christ child, in which the aureole streams toward him, not outward!"

"Splendid!" responded Agnes. "You have struck just the right note, and I could not have put it better. Only the mother, whose love sees the whole man in the child—and this love it is which the angel's greeting[48] acclaims in her—only the mother also sees the heavenly rays already streaming out from him; and only upon her far-seeing face is formed that[49] beautiful reflection which Sophie has represented in the innocent manner of a child. Also, I have recalled this particular evening to you so that you will be able to say better and finer than I, Leonhardt, if only you would.[50] This would be so, for I do not know how to describe with words how deeply and ardently I then felt that all radiant, serene joy is religion; that love, pleasure, and devotion are tones

46. Ed. note: Acts 10:47: "Can any one forbid water for baptizing these people who have received the Holy Spirit just as we have?"

47. In 1806: "pleasure."

48. Ed. note: Luke 1:28–38; "Hail, O favored one, the Lord is with you . . ."

49. In 1806: "the."

50. In 1806: "Leonhardt, or even say at all."

making up a perfect harmony, tones that fit in with each other in any phrasing and in full chord. So if you would do justice to this, Leonhardt, take care you do not scoff; for the truth will fly back at you just as surely as before!"

"Why should I?" retorted Leonhardt. "You have already suggested how you would have it expressed yourself, namely, not with words but in music. However, Friederike, as it appears, has been only listening and has given us nothing to listen to—not even that symbol with which you were so enraptured just now—the simple, fundamental chord. What are we to make of that?"

Friederike

"Oh, well," said Friederike, "it is easier to accompany a narrative like the previous one as it goes along—especially if one already knows something about it," she added, smiling. "Irrespective of that, however, I believe my art will be the less lost on you all if I play only after the story is finished; and that can be done now, if you so desire."

She proceeded to improvise, interweaving some clear, resplendent themes of church music, which are, however, little heard nowadays.[51] And then, to finish once more with her fa-

51. Ed. note: These very words were something of a presentiment, as it turned out. Out of a great interest in church music, which had surfaced early in his life while he was lodged in Herrnhuter Brethren schools, from 1812 to 1829 Schleiermacher had his publisher, Georg Reimer, prepare hymnsheets for use in morning worship at the Dreifaltigkeitskirche (Church of the Triune God). He was a full-time pastor there from 1809 until his death in February 1834. Schleiermacher assembled and reworked these hymns himself, and ordinarily the sheets were printed every two weeks from 1814 through 1828. In the period from 1814 to 1829 he chaired and was the chief contributor to the Gesangbuchkommisssion, appointed by the Berliner Synode. The result was a hymnbook that became quite famous and was widely used. The first edition ran to 662 pages. For the second edition of 1831, fifty

vorite poet, she sang some stanzas from one of Novalis's hymns: "Where stayest thou, world's Consoler, still? / Long waits the room which thou must fill," naturally selecting those which most appeal to feminine understanding.[52]

> O Father, send him forth with power;
> Give from thy hand this richest dower;
> But pureness, love, and shame divine
> Have long kept back this child of thine . . .
>
> The winter wanes; a new year nigh
> Stands by his crib, an altar high;
> It is the whole world's first New Year,
> That with this child doth now appear.
>
> Dim eyes behold the Saviour true,
> The Saviour lights those eyes anew;
> His head the fairest flowers adorn,
> From which he shines like smiling morn.
>
> He is the star; he is the sun;
> The fount whence streams eternal run;
> From herb and stone and sea and light,
> Shines forth his radiant vision bright.

---

thousand copies were printed, followed by fifty thousand each in 1840 and 1847, and two hundred thousand in 1853. See Ilsabe Seibt's full account, *Friedrich Schleiermacher und das Berliner Gesangbuch von 1829* (Göttingen: Vandenhoeck & Ruprecht, 1998).

52. Ed. note: No verses were included in Schleiermacher's text. The hymn first appeared in English in the book *Hymns and Thoughts on Religion by Novalis, with a Biographical Sketch,* translated and edited by W. Hastie (Edinburgh: T. & T. Clark, 1888), as the first among the *Spiritual Songs* he included there. I have used Hastie's text. For the much-longer, original poem, see the Wasmuth edition, 432–33, or the Minor edition, 81–82 (both cited in note 29 above).

Through all things gleams his infant play;
Such warm young love will ne'er decay;
He twines himself, unconscious, blest,
With endless power to every breast . . .

Where verses were left out, she was able to fill[53] the space with harmonies expressing the inner peace, the delight, with which she was stirred and which she wished to represent.

Karoline

"But now, Friederike," announced Karoline, "you must be prepared to make a bridge to the tones of tugging sadness and longing,[54] unless, that is, you would not choose to end with this pure joy, but would have a sketch also from me within the frame of the Christmas festival. It is indeed in my heart to tell you how I began the season last year, in the home of my dear friend Charlotte.[55] Actually there isn't any proper story in it; it is only a supplement to whatever you may have known of Charlotte from other accounts and from her letters, and you must try to recall everything you already know of her.

"In that area, the grownups have the clever custom of bestowing gifts without letting the giver be known. Each person arranges to have one's gift come to another by the longest detours

53. In 1806: "she filled." Ed. note: As Patsch, KGA I/5 (1995) indicates, apparently the more sexually tinged stanzas would have been omitted.

54. *Tönen der Wehmuth.*

55. Ed. note: The story refers to a like experience of his friend Charlotte Sophie von Kathen, born in Mühlenfels (1777–1850), sister of his wife, Henriette (1788–1840). Schleiermacher had come to know them both at their homes on the Isle of Rügen in the Baltic Sea. Schleiermacher married Henriette on May 18, 1809—two years after she had lost her husband, Ehrenfried von Willich (1777–1807), one of Schleiermacher's closest friends.

and in the most peculiar ways, wherever possible hiding it under something less significant, so that the recipient sometimes exclaims and marvels at the gift before finding the real one. Naturally, this requires a great deal of scheming, and the gleeful plan is often not put into operation without long, complicated preparations. Now, for several weeks Charlotte had had to bear the suffering of an inexplicable and thus all the more distressing illness of her little boy, her youngest and most favored child. For a long time, the doctor could as little give as take away hope of recovery; but pain and discomfort continued to rob the little cherub of his strength as time passed, until there was nothing left but to await his death.[56] Among her male and female friends[57] all preparations for surprising the mother by ingenious ploys and mischievous tricks were quietly suspended. No one would venture, even if it were by a simple gift, to distract her from preoccupation with the object of her love and grief. Everything was put off to a time more fitting.

"She carried the child about in her arms almost interminably. Never would she fully retire for the night; only on occasion during the day, when the child seemed quieter and she could give him over to me or to some other intimate friend, would she allow herself a modicum of rest. Nevertheless, she did not neglect the concerns of the Christmas season, though we often bade her not to exhaust herself further with affairs that contrasted so with her own cares. To work herself was, of course, impossible; but she devised and arranged for things, and she often startled me by asking, in the midst of deepest distress, whether this or that was being looked after, or by bringing up some new little enjoyment we could provide for. Of mirth or mischief there was none, only that is not generally her manner anyway.[58] Never, however,

---

56. *Auflösung* ("release").

57. *Unter Freunden und Freundinnen.*

58. In 1806: "there was none."

was there any want of sense for what would be meaningful and important, nor was there any diminishment of that calm grace which is her normal bearing. I still remember that when I once marveled at this behavior, almost disapprovingly, she said to me:

'My good young friend,[59] there is no finer or more befitting frame to put about a painful burden than a chain of small pleasures prepared for others. In this way, everything is placed in a setting in which it can remain for life, and why shouldn't one wish to enter into it at once? There is something out of tune in all that time effaces, and that it surely does with what is vehement in our experience or overly sharp or flat.'

"A few days before Christmas, one could notice that a fierce struggle was going on within her. Almost alone she had remained unconvinced of the child's hopeless condition. Now at last his wan appearance and his weakness had stricken her. The distinct image of death now loomed before her. Withdrawn deeply within herself, for an hour she paced up and down, up and down, with the child in her arms, to all appearances in utter agony. Then, her face flushed with sadness, she gazed at him for a long while[60] as if for the last time, and bending down she placed her lips long against his forehead. Then, gathering her strength and courage, she grasped my hand and said to me:

'Dear friend, now I have overcome it. I have given the little cherub over to the care of heaven from whence he came. I now look calmly for his death, calmly and with a certainty. Yes, I can even wish to see him soon depart, so that the marks of pain and ruin may not distort the angelic picture that has impressed itself so deeply and irrevocably upon my soul.'

"On the morning before Christmas, she gathered the children about her and asked them whether they wanted to celebrate

59. *Mein Kind.* Ed. note: Friederike was quite a bit younger, and thus could be addressed as "child."

60. In 1806: "she gazed at him."

the festival that evening. All was ready and it was up to them. Or they could wait until Eduard had been buried and the first shock and pain had passed. They all declared that they couldn't really enjoy anything just then, but that their little brother was still alive and maybe he would not even die.[61] That afternoon Charlotte gave the child over to me and lay down to rest, and she fell into a deep, refreshing sleep from which I determined I would not awaken her no matter what happened. During the afternoon the frail, dying body underwent a crisis, with violent convulsions, which I took for the last. When the doctor came, he said it could be the final ill or the cure. After about an hour, the child was found to be decidedly better, and one could clearly see that he was on the way to recovery. Swiftly the children decorated the room and wove flowers about the little one's crib.

"When their mother entered, for an instant she thought we had only wished to embellish the appearance of the child's dead body. Then, as she looked over the side of his crib, the first smile of her baby gleamed up at her. Among the flowers, he seemed to her like a drooping bud that had raised its head after a refreshing rain and tugged within to blossom. Once she had learned all that had happened, she embraced us all and said:

'If it is not a delusive hope, this is a regeneration different from that I had expected. I had hoped and prayed,' she added, 'that the child might be raised from his earthly life during these festive days. It was sad but soothing to think of sending a cherub to heaven at the time when we celebrate the sending to earth of the most preeminent of all. Now both of them come to me alike, bestowed directly from God. On the festival of the rebirth of the world, my precious child is born to a new life. Yes, he will live,[62] there is no doubt of it,' she said as she bent over him, scarcely daring to stir him and pressing his tiny hand to her lips. 'May he

61. In 1806: "and surely would not die."

62. Ed. note: The boy referred to did live: Gottlieb Ferdinand Ehrenfried von Kathen (22 May 1804—10 October 1854).

continue to be[63] such a little angel,' she said after a while, 'purified by the pain as though he had[64] passed triumphant through death and had[65] been consecrated to a higher life. He is to me a special[66] gift of grace, a heavenly child, because I had already given him over to heaven."'

Karoline felt impelled to relate even more exact details of her story and of the rare excellence of her friend, for whom she had[67] an especially devoted regard. Leonhardt listened with intent interest, and he was virtually annoyed when Ernst asked him: "But don't you find the same thing here as before—an inverted Mary, as it were, who begins with the most profound maternal suffering, the *Stabat Mater*,[68] and ends with rejoicing over the divine child?"

"Or perhaps there is no reversal at all," said Ernestine. "Consider that indeed Mary's pain could not but vanish in her feeling for the divine eminence and glory of her son, just as from the very beginning, in view of her faith and her hopes, everything that externally confronted him could appear to her only as suffering, as separation."

At this point, the company was invaded by a roving patrol of acquaintances, and the conversation was interrupted. Some of the party belonged to no particular circle. Some, being of a restless frame of mind, had gone through their own sources of enjoyment more quickly and were now roaming about, look-

63. In 1806: "He continues to be."

64. In 1806: "purified by the pain, he has."

65. In 1806: "has."

66. *Vorzügliches Gnadengeschenk*; in 1806: *Gesonderes Gnadengeschenk*.

67. In 1806: "has."

68. Ed. note: With these words begins the traditional hymn in the Latin church recognizing the seven sufferings of Mary (literally: his "mother" was "standing" by the cross—see John 19:25).

ing in here and there to see how others were doing. In order to be more welcome onlookers, and to find a friendly reception wherever they went, they announced themselves as Christmas elves[69] and distributed the choicest, tastiest dainties among the boys and girls. Sophie was spared the usual ceremony of inquiring about the children's behavior, thus gladly attached herself forthwith to the new arrivals. She quickly relighted her display and was as informative a hostess as she was a curious inquisitor about everything they had seen elsewhere. Meanwhile food was quickly handed round, and the visitors soon hastened away. As they left, they invited any to join them who wished, but this Eduard would not allow. They must all remain together a while longer, he said;[70] and besides, Josef was certainly to be expected, and he had been promised that he should find them all there.

69. Ed. note: Actually there are none of the woodland creatures called elves in the German Christmas tradition. The function of the *Weihnachtsknechte* referred to here was to aid Knecht Ruprecht, Saint Nicholas's lieutenant. Translated into English and American tradition, they are Santa's helpers: Christmas elves.

70. In 1806: "awhile longer."

4

On the Meaning of Christmas

When the visitors had departed,[1] Ernst said: "Well, since it has been decided that we should wait the evening out here in conversation and refreshment, I think we men owe the women something in return, so that they may be the more willing to stay with us. Storytelling is not the gift of men, however. At any rate, I know how very little I should be expected to produce myself. Instead, what would you think if we were to follow the English fashion, not to say the Greek,[2] of selecting a topic upon which each person is obliged to say something? Indeed, this custom is not altogether strange among us either. Moreover, we could indeed choose a subject, and a mode of discussing it, by which we would not be led to forget the women's presence in any sense but would consider it our finest achievement to be understood and approved by them."

All agreed, and the women expressed special pleasure, because they had not heard the like for a long time.

1. In 1806: "dispersed."

2. In 1806: "that of the ancients." This form of dialogue or debate, carried by several successive speakers, is especially reported in Plato's *Symposium*. Within Schleiermacher's series of Plato translations, the first volume of which had appeared in 1804, the last in 1828, the *Symposium* was to be included in one to be published in 1807.

Leonhardt

"All right, then," Leonhardt insisted, "since you women are taking such an interest in the proposal, you must also give us the topic upon which we are to speak. Otherwise we may clumsily lay hold of something all too farfetched or indifferent[3] to your taste."

"If the others are of the same mind," Friederike "said, "and if it wouldn't be too annoying to you, Leonhardt, I should like to propose Christmas itself as your topic, for it is this which holds[4] us together here tonight. It has so many aspects to it that each person can easily extol it as he likes best."

No one made any objection to this. Ernestine remarked[5] that any other subject would have been strange indeed and would in a way have disrupted the entire evening.

"Very well, then," said Leonhardt, "in accordance with our custom, as the youngest present I cannot refuse to be the first speaker. And I assent to this all the more gladly in part because my inadequate attempt can be most readily supplanted by a better one, and in part because I shall most surely enjoy the pleasure of anticipating someone else's first thoughts. I must also note," he smiled, "that your arrangement invisibly doubles the number of speakers. This is so, for you will hardly fail to attend church services tomorrow, and it would indeed redound more to our annoyance than to the joy of the preachers if you had to hear the same thing in church all over again—though to you it would perhaps bring boredom at the very most! Therefore I will withdraw as far as possible from their line of thinking and start off my discourse as follows.

"One can extol and praise a thing in either of two ways: first in commending it, by which I mean acknowledging and present-

3. In 1806: "all too indifferent."

4. In 1806: "has brought."

5. In 1806: "averred."

ing[6] its kind and its inner nature as something good; but then also in honoring it, that is, in giving[7] prominence to its comparative excellence and perfection in its kind. Now, the first may be set aside, or it may be left to others to give a general commendation of the Christmas festival, as such, however much[8] a good it may be that the remembrance of great events should be secured and furthered by certain rites and traditions repeated[9] at appointed seasons. If there are to be such festivals, however, and if the very earliest beginning of Christianity is to be regarded as something of primary importance, then no one can deny that this festival of Christmas is an admirable one. Look how completely it effects its purpose, and under such difficult conditions too!

"Now consider: If a person wanted to say that the remembrance of the Redeemer's birth is[10] far better preserved through Bible study and general instruction in Christianity than through this festival, I should deny it. Why? Because while it might suffice for us who are well educated, as I think, such would by no means be true for the great mass of uneducated folk. Suppose we leave out the Roman Church, where the Scriptures are seldom, if ever, put into their hands, but stick to our own people; it is manifest how little inclined even they are to read the Bible, or prepared even to understand it in its proper context. What does instruction leave imprinted on their memory? Far more the proofs for particular teachings than the story of the Redeemer. And what do they get out of his story by this method? The death of the Redeemer is far more prominently recalled than his first entrance[11] into the world—and out of his life the details that

---

6. In 1806: "commending it or acknowledging."

7. In 1806: "honoring it or giving."

8. In 1806: "festival, however much."

9. In 1806: "rites repeated."

10. In 1806: "this remembrance is."

11. In 1806: "appearance."

an instructor can readily pass on and that lend themselves to imitation.[12]

"In relation to the life of the Redeemer, I would contend that the very ease with which we believe in the miracles presumably performed by him chiefly arises from our festival and the impressions it brings to the fore. I think it's obvious that belief in the miraculous rather arises in this way than through outright witness or doctrine. Otherwise how does it happen that the ordinary Roman Catholic Christian believes so much in the miraculous doings of his saints, even though they border on the absurd, yet would not care to believe in anything similar, however alike it may be represented to be, of personages belonging to an alien religious or historical circle? And why does such a person believe in them, even though the miracles of the saints have no connection at all with the truths and requirements of Christian faith? Clearly, the person believes all this because of the holy days set up to honor the saints. Through such festivals, attitudes that would have no persuasive power in the sheer telling take hold when they are tied up with something forcefully presented to the senses, and their hold is continually strengthened in the same way.

"It's exactly what we find in antiquity, when all sorts of strange things from the dim past were chiefly preserved in this fashion. Festivals instigated belief, belief even in such things as historians and poets say little or nothing of.[13] Indeed, rites so

12. In 1806: "into the world."

13. Ed. note: in 1806 the entire previous paragraph and this one up to here reads as follows. "How much more of this history do the people even experience through festive practices than through written tradition is made clear from the following observations. Don't ordinary Catholic folk know a great deal about the saints, of whom they never read anything, simply because of their observance of saints' days and bound up with the particular assistance they request from each one, even to the point of deriving from this certain distinct concepts of their persons? Moreover, in antiquity wasn't a great deal retained from

much more effectively serve this purpose than words[14] that not infrequently it was for the sake of festive rites and traditions, after their true signification had been lost to view, that false histories were fabricated and even came to be believed. Likewise, we have analogies in the Christian church itself for the converse procedure,[15] in which fables have been devised to augment the miraculous still more, and really come to be believed only when holy days are consecrated to them. The festival of the so-called assumption of the Virgin Mary is such a one.

"If, then, the common folk hold so much more to rites and customs than to narratives and doctrines, we have every reason to believe that in our society belief in the supposedly miraculous events connected with the appearance of the Redeemer is very largely due to our festival and its popular conventions. Accordingly, in the Catholic church all that relates to Mary aids and abets this process, since she is always hailed as the Virgin. So, this consideration, and all that it implies, is the merit for which I honor and praise the festival of Christmas.[16]

"Now, I must explain what I meant by saying that the remembrance of Christmas has been especially difficult to preserve, and that the merit of the Christmas festival is all the

---

previous eras by means of festive occasions, of the details of which historians and poets have little or nothing to say?"

14. In 1806: "Indeed, rites are so much the more effective than words."

15. In 1806: "that not infrequently false histories were fabricated from festive rites the true meaning of which had been lost, but never the reverse procedure."

16. Ed. note: In 1826 all the text between note 15 and this one replaces the following from 1806: "Thus, if the common folk hold more to festive rites than to false histories, we also have to believe that in its broad compass the remembrance of Christ is preserved more through festivals than through writings. This is true precisely among a people who, to speak plainly and simply, take as little profit from him as understanding."

greater because[17] of this. The more that is known of a subject, the more definitely and meaningfully can a presentation of it be made; and the more necessarily it fits together with present experience, the more simply can every provision for its recollection be established. However, all that pertains to the first appearance of Christ seems to me to lack this character entirely.[18] This is so, for while I'll grant, without hesitation, that Christianity is a vigorous contemporary force, the personal activity of Christ on earth seems to me to have far less a connection with it than most people believe. I think that, in fact, they rather more suppose than believe in this connection anyway.[19]

"Specifically, what concerns the reconciliation[20] of the human race through him we all connect with his death first off. That event, however, turns more on an eternal decree of God than on a distinct, particular fact, as I think, and on that account we are rather obliged not to tie these ideas to a particular moment but to extend them beyond the temporal history of the Redeemer and to hold them as symbolic. And yet, it is natural that the notion of remembering both the death of Christ, as the sign of reconciliation fully accomplished, and his resurrection,

17. In 1806: "to preserve because."

18. In 1806: "As it appears however, this is lacking with respect to Christ."

19. In 1806: "force, how little does Christ, the actual person, have any connection with it."

20. *Versöhnung.* Ed. note: In German this word does double duty, sometimes referring only to events focused on Christ's death. From early on, in his sermons and writings Schleiermacher never restricts the word in this way. See his short definition of the Redeemer's "reconciling activity" in *Christian Faith* §101 and his alternatives to most classical views of Christ's "atoning" death in *Christian Faith* §104. On the "one eternal divine decree," alluded to later in this sentence, see the English edition of his 1819 essay *On Election*, edited and translated by Iain G. Nicol and Allan Jorgenson (Louisville: Westminster John Knox, 2011), and *Christian Faith* §§117–20.

as the pledge of it, must be forever fortified among the faithful. Thus, the resurrection was also the chief subject of the earliest proclamation and the foundation upon which the church was built, so that it perhaps wouldn't even have been necessary to have a continual repetition of its remembrance by making Sunday a fixed celebration of it.

"Irrespective of the notion of atonement, however, if we consider the human activity of Christ, whose substance is to be sought in the proclamation of his teaching and in the founding of the Christian community, it is astounding how small a part one can rightly ascribe to him within the present configuration of Christianity. Only think of how little of its doctrine or of its institutions can be traced back to Christ himself. By far the most of it is of some other later origin![21] Suppose we arrange all these in a series: John the forerunner of the Messiah, Christ, the apostles (including the Apostle Paul), then the early fathers. Surely one must admit that Christ does not stand just midway between the first and the third but that he is much closer to John the Baptist than to Paul. Indeed it remains doubtful whether it was at all in accordance with Christ's will that such an exclusive and tightly organized church[22] should be formed, without which Christianity as we know it today[23]—and consequently our festi-

21. Ed. note: In 1826 the text beginning from after note 19 to this point replaces the following from 1806: "Specifically, whatever is taught of reconciliation in Christ, I take exception to its being conceived as a distinct, particular fact, for this too is grounded more in an eternal decree of God and on that account is not stated in one particular moment. Rather, it is to be regarded as lifted above temporal history and held in mythical form. In contrast, as the founder of Christianity— and this is in any case the content of his life and the sole relation in which his first appearance in time can be celebrated—Christ himself has a comparatively meager significance, for how little can be traced back to him. By far the most of it is of a different and later origin!"

22. In 1806: "that a church so separated off."

23. In 1806: "Christianity."

val as well, the subject to which I am to address myself—would be inconceivable.

"Now, for this reason the life of Christ receded far to the background of early proclamation, and, as most people now believe, it was told only fragmentarily and by persons removed from the actual events, by subordinates. Indeed, if one notes the zealous attempt of these early accounts to attach Christ[24] to the old line of Jewish kings—which is nevertheless entirely unimportant, whether the relation holds or not, for the founder of a world religion—then it must be admitted that his life was told only in a subordinate fashion. Christ's supernatural birth, however, seems to have been broadcast through narratives still less; otherwise there could not have been so many Christians at the time who took him to be a man begotten naturally, with the consequence that the truth appears to have been saved from the rubbish heap and to have retained importance only by our festival. This would be so, for of itself the narration would never have sufficed, because of conflicting views. If the narrators took no notice of these differences, they couldn't have got the story straight; if they did take notice, then to a certain extent they would have become party to the different views rather than witnesses and reporters. This is seen in that the divergence of accounts is so great that, however we may designate it, every claim or report undoes

24. Ed. note: In 1806 this paragraph begins: "Moreover, to delve deeper in accordance with the times, Christianity itself got submerged, if one notes the diligent efforts of those who were describing his life to attach him to." Although many of the judgments in Leonhardt's argument throughout this account could also be obtained by using rationalist approaches of the time that Schleiermacher abjured, the gist of it is consistent with his own position, which was derived in part through use of historical-critical methods. The concluding paragraphs are a bridge to views that he maintained in his sermons as an affirmation of a continuing Christian community of faith, but these views were not typically held by rationalists. Moreover, he presented theological grounds, something that Leonhardt seems to shy away from.

the others. Or can anyone claim that the resurrection occurred without having to leave it open for anyone to explain the death of Christ as having never happened?—which indeed can mean nothing else than that a later fact declares a view that has been drawn from earlier facts to be false. Similarly, the ascension of Christ to a certain degree throws suspicion upon the truth of his life.[25] The latter happens, for his life belongs to this planet, and what can be divorced from the same cannot have stood in any vital connection with it.

"Just as little remains if one takes the view of those who deny Christ a true body or the view of those who deny him a true human soul together with the view of people who, on the contrary, will not attribute true deity or even superhumanity to him. Indeed, if one considers the dispute over whether he is still present on earth only in a spiritual[26] and divine way, or in that way and in a bodily, sensible way as well, both parties can easily be carried to the point where the common, hidden meaning in their positions is that Christ was never present back then, or lived an earthly existence among his followers, in any different or more distinctive manner than he does now. In short, what

25. Ed. note: In 1826 the text from "then it must be admitted" to this point replaced the following from 1806: "Thus, it is obvious that the birth and the actual presence of Christ in history coheres very little with Christianity itself. Yet, that we know all too little about him, it might almost be said, bears just as little certitude, for already at the time when the first reports of him were composed, the opinions were so varied that the authors appear to have taken no notice of how these opinions were themselves to a certain extent changed from witnesses and reporters among the various parties. Indeed, it can be said that every report and every claim undoes the others. For example, the resurrection inveighs against the actual occurrence of the death, which indeed can mean nothing else than that a later fact declares a view that has been drawn from earlier facts to be false. In contrast, the ascension throws suspicion on the life."

26. *Geistige.* In 1806: *geistliche.*

might be experienced and historically valid regarding the personal existence of Christ has become so precarious because of the diversity of views and doctrines; therefore if our festival is primarily to be regarded as the basis of a continuing common faith in Christ, it is thereby all the more to be extolled. Moreover, a power is demonstrated within it that borders[27] on what I have already mentioned, namely, that sometimes only through such traditions does history itself come to be made.

"Yet, something else is most to be wondered at in all this—and can serve as an example and reproach with respect to much else. It is that the festival itself evidently owes its prevalence, to a great extent, to the fact that it has been brought into the homes and is celebrated among the children. There is where we ought to fasten down what is valuable and sacred to us, much more than we do. Moreover, we should look on it as a bad sign and a discredit to us that we do not follow the practice of fastening these things down.

"This tradition, therefore, we shall want to maintain as it has been handed down to us; and the less surely we can explain wherein its marvelous power lies, the less eager we will be to change even the least detail in it. For me, at least, even the smallest features are full of meaning. Just as a child is the main object of our celebration, so it is also the children above all who elevate the festival and carry it forth—and through it Christianity itself. Just as night is the historic cradle of Christianity, so the birthday celebration of Christianity is begun at nighttime; and the candles with which it sparkles are, as it were, the star above the inn and the halo without which the child would not be discerned in the darkness of the manger or in the otherwise starless night of history. Finally, just as it is dark and doubtful what we have received in the person of Christ, and from whom we have received the

27. In 1806: "In short, the experiential, historical basis of the matter is so weak that thereby our festival is all the more to be extolled, and its power borders on."

gift, so the custom that I learned of through Karoline's narrative is also the finest way of giving presents at Christmastime, and the most aptly symbolic. This is my honest opinion, upon which I suggest we touch our glasses and empty them in a toast—a toast to an unending continuation of the Christmas festival![28] Furthermore, I am all the more certain of your compliance that I hope thereby to make up for and to wash everything that may have seemed offensive to you in what I have said."

"Now I understand," said Friederike, "why he made so little objection to our proposal. The unbelieving rascal had in mind speaking completely against its actual meaning! I should like to make him pay plenty for this, especially since it is I[29] who proposed the task, and since it could well be said that he has made fun of me by the way he chose to carry it out."

"Perhaps you are right," nodded Eduard. "But it would be hard to get at him; for he has taken care, true attorney that he is, to cover himself by prior explanation and by the way he has fused his disparaging remarks with the intention of exalting the Christmas festival, as indeed he had to."

"There is certainly nothing wrong with proceeding like an advocate," Leonhardt rejoined, "and why shouldn't I take every opportunity to exercise such portions of my craft as may be fitting and legitimate? Besides, I wouldn't dare say no to the women, and they couldn't have provided anything more appropriate to that mode of thinking, to which I confess openly enough, or for that matter anything that could have avoided it. Yet, in a way, I haven't proceeded as an advocate at all, for nowhere in my discourse have I introduced the slightest appeal for the favor of our fair judges."

"We must also bear you witness," said Ernst, "that you have spared us much that might have been mentioned—whether be-

28. In 1806: "in a toast."
29. In 1806: "since I."

cause you didn't have it at hand, or because you forbore it to save time and so as not to speak too learnedly and unintelligibly before the women."

"For my part," Ernestine said, "I should like to give him credit for so honorably keeping his promise to stay away, as much as possible, from what we might hear in places of worship tomorrow."

"All right, then," yielded Karoline, "if it is not possible to bring him to judgment straightway, then our first recourse is to refute him. And if I am not mistaken, it depends on you, Ernst, to speak up and preserve the honor of our proposal."

Ernst responded: "I do intend to tackle the latter request, but without offering any refutation—and for my part I should not care to have the two joined together. To speak against Leonhardt's notions would distract me from other topics, and then I might become liable to penalty myself. Moreover, for one who is unaccustomed to organized extemporaneous speaking, nothing is more difficult in undertaking it than trying to follow upon another's train of thought."

Ernst

Ernst began: "Before you spoke, Leonhardt, I should not have known whether what I want to say should be labeled 'commending' or 'honoring.' But now I know that in its own way, it is a kind of honoring, for I too want to praise the Christmas festival as excellent in its kind. Unlike you, I shall not, however, leave up in the air whether the specific idea of the festival and its kind are to be commended as something good, but I will rather presuppose this. There is one qualification. Your definition of a festival does not suffice for me. It was one sided, on the whole adapted only to your own requirements. My definition is different, and it proceeds from another direction. That is, while you only took the point of view that every festival is a commemoration of something, what concerns me is the question of what it commemorates. Accordingly, I propose that a festival is founded only to commemorate that through the presentation of which a certain mood and disposition can be aroused within people; and I propose, further, that the excellence of any festival consists in the fact that such an effect is realized within its entire scope, and vividly so.

"The mood that our festival is meant to incite is joy. That this mood is very widely and vividly aroused through the Christmas festival is so obvious that nothing more need be said on that score. Everyone can see for oneself. Yet, there is one difficulty that might be mentioned, and I shall have to remove it. One might say that it is in no way distinctive of the Christmas festival or essential to it that it should produce this effect, which is only incidental, as are the particular presents that are given and received. Now, this claim is plainly false, as I will try to show. Look, if you give children the same gifts at Christmas as you do at another time, you won't evoke even the semblance of Christmas delight—not unless you come to the corresponding point in their own lives, namely, the celebration of their birthdays. I believe I am right in calling this a corresponding point, and certainly no one will deny that the joy at a birthday has quite a different character from that at Christmastime. One's mood on one's birthday has all the intimacy of being confined within a particular set of personal circumstances, while that at Christmastime bears all the fire, the[30] rapid stirring of a widespread, general feeling.[31] From this we then see that in no way is

30. In 1806: "all the fire and the."

31. Ed. note: In 1826 what is presented from this point up to the next-to-last sentence of the fifth paragraph replaces the following text from 1806: "From this we then see that in no way is it the presents that bring out the joy but that they are the occasion for this. On the other hand, we also see that what is distinctive about Christmas joy consists precisely in the totally all-inclusive (*allgemeine*) character it

it the presents in themselves that bring out the joy, but that they are given only because there is already great cause for rejoicing.

---

has. Throughout a great part of Christendom—as far as this fine old custom is still observed—each person is occupied in preparing a gift. This conscious effort consists precisely in its all-pervasive charm.

"A gift incidentally picked up at an ordinary shop or worked on during leisure hours without any further connection is of little or no value. However, the fact that people are planning together for Christmas, working to outdo each other in preparing for the special hours of celebration—and then out-of-doors the Christmas markets, their lights reflecting off each gift just as sparkling little stars gleam in the snowy winter night as if the reflection of heaven were cast upon it—all this gives the presents their value.

"Nor can what is so all-inclusive ever have been arbitrarily devised. Some inner cause must underlie it; otherwise it could not have produced this effect or even continued as it has, as can be seen quite satisfactorily in contrast with many recent attempts that lacked these conditions. This inner feature, however, cannot be other than the very ground of all joy that is stirred up here and there among these people, for no such effect could arise from any other source. Moreover, this is also how it works out. There are those who have attempted to transfer the widespread joy that belongs to the Christmas season to the New Year, that point at which the changes and contrast of time are preeminent. I cannot draw attention to this view without lodging a complaint against it, and for the reason I have just stated. There are those, of course, who, lacking stability of character, live only from year to year and rejoice simply in the renewal of what is transitory. So, the relation between the birth of the Redeemer and this general festival of joy lies precisely in the fact that for all who do not live in the changes of time, as these people do, there is no principle of joy other than redemption, or for a child. Thus, too, no other festival has such a kinship to this all-inclusive festival as that of baptism, unless one goes at it totally failing to grasp its meaning."—Ed. note: For other reasons, Schleiermacher himself also gave the beginning of a New Year a special significance. See, for example, his *Soliloquies*, pegged by him as "a New Year's gift" (forthcoming, translated by Tice). See also *Fifteen Sermons of Friedrich Schleiermacher Delivered to Celebrate the Beginning of a New Year*, edited and translated and introduced by Edwina Lawler (Lewisburg, NY: Mellen, 2003).

And the distinctiveness of Christmas Day, which consists precisely in the great general character it has, also extends itself to the presents, so that throughout a great part of Christendom—as far as this fine old custom is still observed—everyone is occupied in preparing a gift, and in this conscious effort lies a great part of its all-pervasive charm.

"Think what it would be like if only a single family held to this observance whereas all the others in their area had given it up. The impression would no longer be the same—not by a long shot. However, the fact that many people are planning together for it, working to outdo each other in preparing for the special hours of celebration—and then out-of-doors the Christmas markets, open to all and intended for the whole populace, their lights reflecting off each gift just as sparkling little stars gleam from earth in the snowy winter night as if the reflection of heaven were cast upon it—all this gives the presents their special value.

"Nor can what is so all-inclusive have been arbitrarily devised or agreed upon. Rather, some common inner cause must underlie it; otherwise it cannot have produced so similar an effect or even generally survived as it has, as can be seen quite satisfactorily in contrast with many recent attempts that lacked these conditions. This inner ground, however, cannot be other than the appearance of the Redeemer as the source of all other joy in the Christian world; and for this reason nothing else can deserve to be so celebrated as this event.

"Some, to be sure, have attempted to transfer the widespread joy that belongs to the Christmas season to the New Year, the day on which the changes and contrast of time are preeminent. I cannot draw attention to this view without lodging a complaint against it, and for the reason I have just stated. Many people, of course, have followed this practice without thinking, and it would be unfair to claim that wherever gifts are exchanged at the New Year instead of at Christmas people are giving little place to the distinctively Christian element in their lives. Yet, this divergent custom is connected plainly enough with just such a neglect. The New Year is devoted to the renewal of what is only transitory. Therefore, it is especially appropriate that those who, lacking stability of character, live only from year to year should make an especially joyful day[32] of it.

"All human beings are subject to the shifts of time. That goes without saying. However, some of the rest of us do not desire to have our life in what is only transitory. For us the birth of the Redeemer is the sole all-inclusive festival of joy, precisely because we believe that there is no principle of joy other than redemption. In its progress the birth of the divine child is the first bright spot, and, as a result, we cannot postpone our joy by waiting for another. Thus, too, no other festival has such a kinship to this all-inclusive festival as that of baptism, through which the principle of joy in the divine child is appropriated to the little ones. This also explains the particular fascination of Agnes's charming account, in which the two were conjoined."

"Yes, Leonhardt, look at it as we may, there is no escaping the fact that that original, natural state of vitality and joy in which there are no opposites of appearance and being, time and eternity, is not ours to possess. Furthermore, if we think these to exist in one person then we must think of him as Redeemer, and as one who must start out as a divine child. In contrast, we ourselves begin with the discord between time and eternity, appearance and being. Moreover, we attain to harmony only through redemption, which is nothing other than the overcoming of these oppositions, and which on this account can proceed only from one for whom they have not had to be overcome.

"Certainly no one can deny that. It is the distinctive nature of this festival that through it we should become conscious of an innermost ground out of which a[33] new, untrammeled life emerges, and of its inexhaustible power, that in its very first germ

32. *Freudentag.*
33. In 1806: "the."

we should already discern its finest maturity, indeed its[34] highest perfection. However unconsciously it may reside in many people, our feeling of wonder can achieve resolution only in this concentrated vision[35] of a new world, and in no other way. This vision may grip anyone, and he who brought it into being may be[36] represented in a thousand images and in the most varied ways—as the rising, ever-returning sun, as the springtime of the spirit, as king of a better realm, as the most faithful emissary of the gods, as the prince of peace.

"And so I have come to the point of refuting you after all, Leonhardt, even in noting where we agree and in comparing the different viewpoints from which we have started. However unsatisfactory the historical traces of his life may be when one examines it critically—in a lower sense—nevertheless the festival does not depend on this inquiry. It rests on the necessity of a Redeemer, and hence on the experience of a heightened existence, which can be derived from no other beginning than him. Often you yourself find less of a trace than I do in particles upon which some crystallization of truth has been formed, but even the smallest features have sufficed to convince you that a trace was present. So it is actually Christ to whose powers of attraction this new world owes its formation, and whoever acknowledges Christianity to be a powerful contemporary force, the great pattern of new life—as you too are inclined to do—hallows this festival.[37] One does so not as one who dares not impugn what

34. In 1806: "maturity, its."

35. *Anschauung.*

36. In 1806: "anyone and maybe."

37. Ed. note: From the second sentence in this paragraph to here, 1806 reads: "However weak the historical traces when one thus regards the matter critically—in a lower sense—the festival depends not on that but on the necessary idea of a Redeemer, and for that purpose even these traces would be enough. The greatest crystallization needs only a tiny particle to grow from. Likewise, whatever of this joy breaks

one cannot understand, but in that one fully understands all its particulars—the gifts and the children, the night and the light.

"With this slight improvement, which I wish might also win your favor, I give your proposal for a toast once more. I trust, then, or rather prophesy, that the marvelous festival of Christmas will ever preserve the happy, childlike mood with which it returns to us ever and again. To all who celebrate it, moreover, I wish and foresee that true joy in finding the higher life once more, from which alone all its blessings spring."[38]

"I must beg your pardon, Ernst," said Agnes. "I had feared that I would not understand you at all; but this has not happened, and you have very nicely confirmed that its religious feature is in truth the very nature of the festival. Yet, it would certainly appear, from what has been said previously, as if we women should have less share in the joy because less of that lack of harmony you spoke of is revealed in us. Still, I can account for that well enough for myself."

"Very easily," Leonhardt jumped in. "One could simply say right off—and it is as plain as can be—that women bear everything lightly regarding themselves, and that they strive after little self-gratification, just as their innermost suffering is

---

out from within, it needs only the slightest occasion to put itself into some distinct shape. Thus, whoever acknowledges Christianity to be a powerful contemporary force, the great pattern of new life—as you too would do—hallows this festival."

38. Ed. note: Again the speaker, Ernst, constantly reflects themes and positions dear to Schleiermacher's heart and mind, yet like Leonhardt he does not offer the fully theological account that Schleiermacher had offered elsewhere by 1806 and was to fill out in later sermons and in *Christian Faith*. In part, the men's discourses offer something of a progression in laying out what he would most want to say, along the way giving open-minded credit to alternative positions that he could only partially affirm.

shared suffering,[39] so their joy too is shared joy. You must see to it, however, that you square accounts with the sacred authority of Scripture, to which you would ever remain faithful, and which so clearly points to the women as the first cause of all discord[40] and of all human need for redemption! But if I were Friederike, I would declare war on Ernst[41] for having so thoughtlessly, and without the slightest consideration of his situation, given baptism prominence over betrothal, which, I hope, is also to be regarded as a lovely and joyful sacrament."

"Don't answer him, Ernst," piped Friederike. "He has already answered himself."

"How so?" inquired Leonhardt.

"Why, obviously," countered Ernestine, "in that you did speak of your own situation! But people like you never notice when you mix in your own dear egos. Ernst, however, has set up the distinction very well, and he would no doubt say to you that a betrothal is closer to the enjoyment of a birthday than to the joy of Christmas."

"Or," added Ernst, "if you would have something specifically Christian at this point—that it is more like Good Friday and Easter than Christmas! Now, though, let's put aside all that has preceded and listen to what Eduard has to say to us."

Eduard

In response, Eduard began his discourse, as follows:

"It has already been remarked on a similar occasion, by a better man than I," he said, "that the last one to speak on a topic

---

39. *Leiden Mitleiden ist.*

40. Ed. note: Leonhardt is made to play upon the story in Genesis 3 and its reflection in 1 Timothy 2:14.

41. In 1806: "on him."

this way, no matter what its nature, is in the worst position.[42] That is the situation in which I find myself. For one thing, earlier speakers take the words out of one's mouth; and in this respect you two have certainly not taken much trouble to leave any particulars of the festival to me. The main difficulty, however, is that peculiar echoes continue to resound from each discourse in the minds of their listeners, and this forms an increasing resistance to new ideas, which the final speaker has the greatest difficulty in surpassing. Hence, I must look about for aid, and I must let what I want to say rest on something you already know well and appreciate, so that my thoughts may find entrance into yours more easily.

"Now, Leonhardt has mostly had the more external biographers of Christ in mind, seeking out the historical truth in them. In contrast, I shall turn to the mystical one among the four evangelists, whose account offers very little in the way of particular events. Indeed, the Gospel according to John hasn't any Christmas even, recounted as an external event.[43] Yet, in his heart prevails an everlasting, childlike Christmas joy. He gives us the higher, spiritual view of our festival. In contrast, he begins, as you know: 'In the beginning was the Word, and the Word was with God, and the Word was God . . . In him was life, and the life was the light of men . . . And the word became flesh and dwelt among us [and] we have beheld his glory, glory as of the only Son from the Father.'[44]

42. Ed. note: Plato has Socrates say this in the *Symposium* 198a–199a.

43. In 1806: "Now, while Leonhardt referred to the mythical biographers of Christ throughout and tried to find what was historical among them, I shall turn to the mystical one, in whose account there is almost nothing historical at all. The Gospel according to John hasn't any Christmas even, recounted as an external event."

44. Ed. note: John 1:1, 4, 14. The only sermons published thus far that Schleiermacher preached on these verses were in a series on John

"This is how I prefer to regard the object of this festival: not a child of such and such an appearance, born of this or that parent, here or there, but the Word become flesh, which was God and was with God. The flesh, however, is, as we know, nothing other than our finite, limited, sensory nature, while the Word is thinking, coming to know; and the Word's becoming flesh is therefore the appearing of this original and divine Word in that form. Accordingly, what we celebrate is nothing other than ourselves as whole beings—that is,[45] human nature, or whatever else you want to call it, viewed and known based on the divine principle. Why we must raise up one person alone in whom human nature permits of being presented in this way, and why this union of the divine and the earthly is placed in precisely this one

---

for early-morning services on April 13 and May 11, 1823. However, two others were preached on verses in the prologue (John 1:1–18), on May 5, 1823 and December 5, 1830. For further information see my book *Schleiermacher's Sermons* (Lewiston, NY: Mellen, 1997). See also Catherine L. Kelsey, *Schleiermacher's Preaching, Dogmatics and Biblical Criticism: The Interpretation of Jesus Christ in the Gospel of John*, Princeton Theological Monograph Series 68 (Eugene, OR: Pickwick Publications, 2007).

45. In 1806: "or." Ed. note: This statement has often been cited as though it expresses Schleiermacher's position. It does come very close, but he would never have identified "the Word" so strictly with thinking or with any exclusively cognitive content; nor would he have reduced "God" to "human nature," or reduced "flesh" to our "sensory nature" (*sinnliche Natur*), though he could well have referred to what happened in Christ as fulfillment of a "divine principle," in the sense of that which set the appearance of Christ in motion (the divine decree). Furthermore, although he prominently affirmed John 1:14, he did not tend to utilize the preexistent-logos Christology attributed to the Johannine prologue in formulating his otherwise christocentric theology, which in his view had to be critically reflective of the faith of the Evangelical Church in his time and place and appropriate to its life. Nevertheless, in the remainder of this discourse he would not completely have denied anything that is made to flow from Eduard's somewhat overly restricted characterization here.

person, and already even at birth, not as a later fruit of life—all this can be clarified from this point of view.

"As such, what else is humanity than the very spirit of earth, or life's coming to know in its eternal being and in its ever-changing process of becoming? In such a state there is no corruption in humanity, no fall, and no need of redemption. However, when the individual fastens upon other formations of the earthly environment and seeks one's knowledge in them, for the process of coming to know them dwells in oneself alone: this is only a state of becoming. Then the individual exists in a fallen and corrupt condition, in discord and confusion, and then one can find one's redemption only through the human being as such. One finds redemption, that is, in that the same union of eternal being and of the coming into being of the human spirit, such as it can be manifested on this planet, arises in each person, and thus each contemplates and learns to love all becoming, including oneself, only in eternal being. Moreover, insofar as one appears as a process of becoming, one wills to be nothing other than a thought of eternal being; nor will one have one's foundations in any other expression of eternal being[46] than in that which is united with the ever-changing, ever-recurrent process of becoming. Indeed, for this reason the union of being and becoming is found in humanity eternally, because that union exists and comes into being eternally, as the human as being as such does. In the individual person, however, this union—as it has reality in one's own life— must also come into being both as one's own thinking and as the thinking that arises within a common life and activity with other

46. In 1806: "One finds redemption, that is, in that the same union of eternal being and of the coming into being of the spirit of earth arises in a given person, so that one contemplates and learns to love all becoming, including oneself, and so that since one appears as a process of becoming, one wills to be nothing other than a thought of eternal being, nor will one have one's foundations in any other expression of eternal being."

persons; for it is in community that whatever cognition is proper to our planet[47] not only exists but develops. Only when a person sees humanity as a living community of individuals, cultivates humanity as a community, bears its spirit and consciousness in one's life, and within that community both loses one's isolated existence and finds it again in a new way—only then does that person have the higher life and peace of God within oneself.

"Now, this community by which the human being as such is thus exhibited or restored is the church. The church, by virtue of this relation, relates itself to all other human life around it and without, somewhat as the self-consciousness of humanity relates to what lacks consciousness. Everyone, therefore, in whom this genuine self-consciousness of humanity arises enters within the bounds of the church. This is why no one can truly and vitally possess the fruits of science who is not oneself within the church, and why such an outsider can deny the church only externally but not deep within oneself. On the other hand, there may very well be those within the church who do not possess science for themselves, for these can own that higher self-consciousness in immediate experience, even if not in their perspective on things.[48] This is exactly the case with women and, at the same time, the reason why they are so much more fervently and unreservedly attached to the church.

"This community, furthermore, is not only something that is coming into being but also something that has come

47. In 1806: "terrestrial cognition." Ed. note: Regarding the "spirit of the earth" allusion, Kurt Nowak (2001, 172), explains that in this use of the metaphor, "Schleiermacher's subsequent Christology is sketchily announced," though "he did foreswear any use of the 'pansophical'" sort introduced by Friedrich Wilhelm Joseph von Schelling (1775–1854) and Novalis (Georg Friedrich Philipp Freiherr von Hardenberg [1772–1801]).

48. *Denn sie konnen jenes höhere Selbstbewuztsein in der Empfindung besitzen, wenn auch nicht in der Anschauung.* Ed. note: In 1826 *Anschauung* replaces *Erkenntnis* ("knowledge").

into being, and it is also, as a community of individual persons, something that has come into being through communication of persons with one another. Thus, we also seek for a single starting point from which this communication can proceed—though we recognize that it must further proceed from each person out of one's own self-initiated activity—so that the human being as such may also be born and formed in each one.[49] However, the person who is regarded to be the starting point of the church, its originating conception, must already be the human being as such, the person of God, from[50] birth—this person must bear that process of self-knowing[51] in oneself and be the light of all human beings from the very beginning. Analogously, one may, as it were, call the first free, spontaneous outbreak of community of sensory experience at Pentecost,[52] the birth of the church. This is shown in that it is indeed through the Spirit of the church that we are born again. The Spirit itself, however, proceeds only from the Son, and the Son needs no rebirth but is born of God originally. He is the Son of Man without qualification.[53] Until he entered history, all else was presage: all human life was related to his life, and only through this relation did it partake of goodness and divinity. Indeed, now[54] that he has come, in him we celebrate not only ourselves but all who are yet to come as well as all who

49. In 1806: "and the human being as such be born and formed in each one."

50. *Gottmensch.*

51. *Selbsterkennen.*

52. In 1806: "of a community of sensory experience" (*Gemeïnschaft der Empfindung*). Ed. note: As literally "sensation," the experience of sensing. *Empfindung* is reception of what is sensed. Correspondingly, *Empfindlichkeit* is "receptivity" in Schleiermacher's usage, in contrast to *Selbsttätigkeit*, "self-initiated activity" or "spontaneity."

53. *Menschensohn schlechthin.*

54. In 1806: "Moreover."

have been before us, for they were something only insofar as he was in them and they in him.[55]

"In Christ, then, we see the Spirit, according to the nature and means of our world,[56] originatively forming itself to the point of self-consciousness in individual persons. In him, the Father and the brethren[57] dwell equally and are one. Devotion and love are Christ's very nature. Thus it is that every mother who, profoundly feeling what she has done in bearing a human being, knows, as it were by an annunciation from heaven, that the spirit of the church, the Holy Spirit, dwells within her. As a result, she forthwith presents her child to the church with all her heart, and she claims permission to do this as her right.[58] Such a woman also sees Christ in her child—and this is that inexpressible feeling a mother has which compensates for all else. In like manner, however,[59] each one of us beholds in the birth of Christ one's own higher birth whereby nothing lives in oneself but devotion and love, and the eternal Son of God appears in each of us too. Thus it is that the festival breaks forth like a heavenly light out of the darkness. Thus it is that a pulse of joy spreads out over the whole reborn world, a pulse that only those who are long ill or maimed of spirit do not feel, and this is the very glory of the festival, which you wished also to hear me praise.

"Ah! But I see I shall not be the last. For our long-awaited friend has come, and he must have his say as well."

---

55. In 1806: "all who have come before us."

56. In 1806: "we see the spirit of the earth."

57. *Brüder.* Ed. note: In Schleiermacher's usage, as with the actual Brethren among whom he had his early schooling, this term refers to females and males alike.

58. In 1806: "in her heart and claims this as a right."

59. In 1806: "In like manner, moreover."

Josef

Josef had come in while he was talking, and although he had very quietly entered and taken a seat, Eduard[60] had noticed him.

"By no means," he replied when Eduard addressed him. "You shall certainly be the last. I have come not to deliver a speech but to enjoy myself with you; and I must quite honestly say that it seems to me odd, almost folly even, that you should be carrying on with such exercises, however nicely you may have done them. Aha! But I already get the drift. Your evil principle is among you again: this Leonhardt, this contriving, reflective, dialectical, superintellectual man. No doubt you have been addressing yourselves to him, for on your own you would surely not have needed such goings-on, and wouldn't have fallen into them. Yet, they couldn't have been to any avail with him! Furthermore, the poor women must have had to go along with it. Now, just think what lovely music they could have sung for you, in which all the piety of your discourse could[61] have dwelt far more profoundly. Or think how charmingly they might have conversed with you, out of hearts full of love and joy. Such would have eased and refreshed you differently than you could possibly have been affected by[62] these celebratory discourses of yours!

"For my part, today I am of no use for such things at all. For me, all forms are too rigid, all speech making too tedious and cold. Itself unbounded by speech, the subject of Christmas claims, indeed creates in me a speechless joy, and I cannot but laugh and exult like a child. Today all human beings are children to me, and are all the dearer to me on that account.[63] The solemn wrinkles are for once smoothed away; the years and cares do not stand written on the brow. Eyes sparkle and dance again, the sign

60. In 1806: "he."
61. In 1806: "would."
62. In 1806: "have been by"
63. In 1806: "and are so dear to me for that reason."

of a beautiful and serene existence within. To my good fortune, I too have become just like a child again. As a child stifles childish pain, suppressing sighs and holding back tears, when something is done to arouse childish joy, so it is with me today. The long, deep, irrepressible pain in my life is soothed as never before. I feel at home, as if born anew into the better world, in which pain and grieving have no meaning and no room any more.[64] I look upon all things with a gladsome eye, even what has most deeply wounded me. As Christ had no bride but the church, no children but his friends, no household but the temple and the world, and yet his heart was full of heavenly love and joy, so I too seem to be born to endeavor just after such a life.[65]

"So, I have roamed about the whole evening, everywhere taking part most heartily in every little happening and amusement I have come across. I have laughed, and I have loved it all. It was one long affectionate kiss that I have given to the world, and now my enjoyment with you shall be the last impress of my lips, for you know that you are the dearest of all to me.

"Come, then, and above all bring the child, if she is not yet asleep, and let me see your glories, and let us be glad and sing something religious[66] and joyful!"

64. Ed. note: The allusion is to Revelation 21:4.

65. In 1806: "so do I seem to be born to endeavor after such a life."

66. *Frommes.* Ed. note: Although there is perhaps nothing special about the name Josef here, unless it is imaginatively reflective of Mary's Joseph, Patsch KGA I/5 (1995) may be correct in recalling "Bruder Joseph," as Bishop August Gottlieb Spangenberg (1704–1792) was called within the Herrnhuter Brethren community. Spangenberg, after its founder, Count Nicolaus Ludwig von Zinzendorf (1700–1760), and according to the customary discourse of the community, could easily have spoken this way. Schleiermacher—dropping off their typical, more specifically pietistic images—could do so more readily still. Joseph's remarks alone among the men's discourses here are a pure mirror image of Schleiermacher's own views and sentiments, as of his own known experiences of suffering, love, and joy at that moment in his life.

Bibliographical Note

Among the several major interpretations of this book, by 1990 four were available in English: (1) Karl Barth's 1924 article, "Schleiermacher's Celebration of Christmas," in *Theology and Church: Shorter Writings, 1920–1928*, a collection of his essays translated by Louise Pettibone Smith and introduced by T. F. Torrance (London: SCM, 1962), 136–58; see also Karl Barth, "Christmas," in his book *The Theology of Schleiermacher: Lectures at Göttingen, Winter Semester of 1923/24*, edited by Dietrich Ritschl, translated by Geoffrey W. Bromiley (Grand Rapids: Eerdmans, 1982), 50–77, which places *Christmas Eve* in the setting of the Christmas sermons; (2) "The Christmas Dialogue," chapter 1 in Richard R. Niebuhr's *Schleiermacher on Christ and Religion: A New Introduction* (New York: Scriber, 1964), 21–71; (3) Terrence N. Tice, "Schleiermacher's Interpretation of Christmas: 'Christmas Eve,' 'The Christian Faith,' and the Christmas Sermons," *Journal of Religion* 47 (1967) 100–26; also the "Introduction," "Dramatis Personae," and "Notes" in the 1967 edition of this work, 7–24, 87–89, somewhat revised in the 1990 edition; and (4) Ruth Drucilla Richardson, "Christmas Eve: A Conversation (1806)," chapter 6 in her book, *The Role of Women in the Life and Thought of the Early Schleiermacher (1768–1806): An Historical Overview* (Lewiston, NY: Mellen, 1990), in part drawn from her 1985 Drew University dissertation, which centered on *Christmas Eve*. Aspects of the dialogue had also been interpreted, for the most part affirmatively, in two other pieces: (5) Brian A. Gerrish, *A Prince of the Church: Schleiermacher and the Beginnings of Modern Theology*, The Rockwell Lectures 1981 (Philadelphia: Fortress, 1984), 27–31, 46–47; and (6) Dawn

DeVries, "Schleiermacher's *Christmas Eve Dialogue*: Bourgeois Ideology or Feminist Theology?" *Journal of Religion* 69 (1989) 169–83.

Barth (1924) chiefly argues against the kind of position Niebuhr (1964) later advocated in favor of Schleiermacher's purported views. The Tice essay (1967), an analytic companion to the present introduction (1967, somewhat revised in 1990 and currently), includes a critique of these and other interpretations, a detailed historical and doctrinal analysis of the dialogue, and a comparative study of the Christmas sermons. Richardson, *The Role of Women* (1990), offers important background, demonstrates parallels between the women's stories and the men's speeches, and weaves into her monograph Schleiermacher's views on women, views that were on the whole strikingly advanced for his time. There she also draws comparisons with ideas he presented in earlier works: in *Versuch einer Theorie des geselligen Betragens*, in *Vertraute Briefe*, in *Brouillon zur Ethik*, and in the *Reden*. (Almost all his most significant early works are now available in English translation.) Among earlier perspectives she finds helpful, though problematic, are the two post-Barth German accounts by Emanuel Hirsch, in his book *Schleiermachers Christusglaube: Drei Studien* (Gütersloh: Mohn, 1968); and by Erwin H. U. Quapp, *Barth contra Schleiermacher? "Die Weihnachtsfeier" als Nagelprobe mit einem Nachwort zur Interpretationgeschichte der "Weihnachtsfeier"* (Marburg: Wenzel, 1978).

Four very helpful contributions on the early reception of *Christmas Eve* and on some of its structural features come from Hermann Patsch: (1) "Die zeitgenössische Rezeption der 'Weihnachtsfeier,'" in *Internationaler Schleiermacher-Kongreß Berlin 1984*, edited by Kurt-Victor Selge, *Schleiermacher-Archiv* Bd. 1/2 (Berlin: de Gruyter, 1985), 1215–28; (2) "Die esoterische Kommunikationsstruktur der *Weihnachtsfeier*: Über Anspielungen und Zitate," in *Schleiermacher in Context: Papers from the 1988 International Symposium on Schleiermacher at Hernnhut, the German Democratic Republic,* edited by Ruth Drucilla Richardson (Lewiston, NY: Mellen, 1990), 132–58; (3) "Taufe in Schleiermachers 'Wiehnachtsfeier' (Agnes's Story)," in *CA—Confessio Augustana* 4 (2001) 64–66; and (4) "Die 'mimische' *Weihnachtsfeier*: Überlegungen zu einen unsicheren Lesung" [Friedrich Schlegel's], 159–64, in Hans Dierkes, Terrence N. Tice, and Wolfgang Virmond, editors, *Schleiermacher, Romanticism and the Critical Arts: A Festschrift in Honor of Hermann Patsch, New Athenaeum/Neues Athenäum* 8 (Lewiston, NY: Mellen, 2007). Highly important additions to an understanding of this work already appeared at the hands of Hermann Patsch in his critical edition of the *Weihnachtsfeier* in *Kritische Gesamtausgabe* (KGA) I/5 (1995), 39–100, and in his "Historische Einführung," xlii–lxvii. A more recent account of *Christmas Eve* in its historical setting is given by Kurt Nowak in his excellent biography: *Schleiermacher: Leben, Werk und Wirkung* (Göttingen: Vandenhoeck & Ruprecht, 2001), 163–73. See also Patsch (2006) below.

The following works, arranged from earliest to latest publication date, make up a particularly significant literature:

(1) Patricia E. Guenther-Gleason, *On Schleiermacher and Gender Politics*, Harvard Theological Studies 43 (Harrisburg, PA: Trinity, 1997).

(2) Patricia E. Guenther-Gleason, "'Christmas Eve' as a Work of Art: Implications for Interpreting Schleiermacher's Gender Ideology," in Ruth Drucilla Richardson and Edwina Lawler, editors, *Understanding Schleiermacher: From Translation to Interpretation; A Festschrift in Honor of Terrence Nelson Tice*, Schleiermacher Studies and Translations 16 (Lewiston, NY: Mellen, 1998), 117–62.

(3) Bernd-Holger Janssen, *Die Inkarnation und das Werden der Menschheit: Eine Interpretation der Weihnachtspredigten Friedrich Schleiermachers im Zusammenhang mit seinem philosophisch-theologischen System*, Marburger theologische Studien 79 (Marburg: Elwert, 2003).

(4) Lori Pearson, "Schleiermacher and the Christologies behind Chalcedon," *Harvard Theological Review* 96 (2003) 349–67.

(5) Andries G. van Aarde, "Die ou-Kersaandsgesprek van Friedrich Schleiermacher in Afrikaans: agtergrund, vertaling en hermeneutic," *Hervormde teologiese studies* 59 (2003) 545–68. [Translation of the first part of Schleiermacher's *Christmas Eve,* with introduction in Afrikaans.]

(6) Heleen Zorgdrager, *Theologie die verschil maakt: taal en sekse-differentie als sleutels tot Schleiermachers denken* (Zoetermeer: Boekencentrum, 2003).

(7) Elisabeth Hartlieb, *Geschlechterdifferenz im Denken Friedrich Schleiermachers,* Theologische Bibliothek Töpelmann 136 (Berlin: de Gruyter, 2004).

(8) Michael D. Ryan, "Friedrich Schleiermacher's Reinvention of the Christian Faith: *Die Weihnachtsfeier* as a Vision of Christian Humanism," in *The State of Schleiermacher Scholarship Today: Selected Essays,* Edwina Lawler et al., editors (Lewiston, N.Y.: Mellen, 2006), 333–66 [a Festschrift for Michael Ryan; see his explanation of how this essay arose on pages 24–26].

(9) Philip Stolzfus, *Theology as Performance: Music, Aesthetics, and God in Western Thought* (New York: T. & T. Clark, 2006). [On *Christmas Eve,* see especially pages 77–87.]

(10) Hermann W. Patsch, "Verspätete Frühromantik: Friedrich Schleiermacher's 'Weihnachtsfeier,'" in *Schleiermacher-Tag 2005: Eine Vortragsreihe* (Göttingen: Vandenhoeck & Ruprecht, December 2006), 55–64. Patsch's major new philological-literary analysis of this "novella" (a) underscores my own view that Schleiermacher's distinctive contribution to the "early-Romantic movement" in Germany (ca. 1796–1802) lay in his religious and ethical perspectives, and (b) augments my view in showing that in *Christmas Eve Celebration* (1806) he both fulfilled Friedrich Schlegel's principles for *Poesie* (in *Athenäum,* 1800) better than did any of the other major Romantics and markedly improved on those principles, but (c) did so in ways none of these men approved of by 1806. Thus, this work was coming "too late."

Further, Patsch shows (d) that the work has no predecessor or prototype (*Vorbild*)—not even in its constant aesthetic touches, visual and musical. Yet, (e) it not only possesses the "experimental nature" of early-Romantic literary works but also affords a glimpse into the history of 19th century novellas. (f) Thereby, in part, it fulfills the idea in Schlegel's notebook "fragment" that "every progressive man carries . . . a novel . . . within him that expresses the very nature of his life" (58), as Schleiermacher himself had thought of doing but had put off. (g) Patsch does give some comparative attention to several models—but no typology—for presenting a "dialogue" (*Gespräch, Dialog*) with which Schleiermacher was acquainted, including his own attempts before 1796 and Schlegel's rather faulty *Lucinda*, with which he critically compares Schleiermacher's *Weihnachtsfeier* (62f). Finally, (h) Patsch contests this richly accoutered dialogue's reputation as a chiefly "theological" work, considering it to be also a seminal "work of art," as only Schelling (1807), among leading figures who still identified themselves as "Romantics," saw at that time.

A somewhat different perspective on overlapping issues appeared in Schleiermacher's 1818 sermonic treatise, *The Christian Household: A Sermonic Treatise,* translated with essays and notes, by Dietrich Seidel and Terrence N. Tice (Lewiston, NY: Mellen, 1991).

Translations of Schleiermacher's entire dialogue *Christmas Eve Celebration*, with introductions, have recently appeared in several languages. Works on his Christology, on his approach to gender issues, and on his thought and practice regarding music are also regularly appearing, especially in German and English. For a complete listing of the literature on related subjects, see my *Schleiermacher Bibliography* (1966) and *Schleiermacher Bibliography, 1784–1984: Updating and Commentary* (Princeton: Princeton University Press, 1985), and further updates beginning with the 1989, 1991 and 1995 issues of *New Athenaeum/ Neues Athenäum* (published by Edwin Mellen Press). A comprehensive, fully indexed bibliography from 1789 through 2010 is in preparation (Tice, forthcoming).

Apart from Charles Dickens's *A Christmas Carol* and collections of Christmas hymns and carols, it would appear that no literature on the Christmas festival comparable to Schleiermacher's *Christmas Eve Celebration* exists. Nor, apart from Schleiermacher's work, has any prominent comprehensive theological interpretation of Christmas been found that might be recommended to the general reader.

Index

As befits Sophie's candied "dainties" and the numerous "particulars" of Christmas in this dialogue, what follows is a finely textured index of names, themes, and expressions. The index includes sections on the *dramatis personae* and an attempt at distinguishing four modes of "dialogue" displayed in this work.

The Scripture Index is placed at the end.

Index

Index

Index

Scripture Index

Lightning Source UK Ltd.
Milton Keynes UK
UKOW03f0637160314

228208UK00002B/75/P